The Sea Island's Secret

Young Palmetto Books

Kim Shealy Jeffcoat, Series Editor

The
Sea Island's
SECRET

A Delta & Jax Mystery

Susan Diamond Riley

THE UNIVERSITY OF
SOUTH CAROLINA PRESS

Published by the University of South Carolina Press
Columbia, South Carolina 29208

www.sc.edu/uscpress

Manufactured in the United States of America

28 27 26 25 24 23 22 21 20 19
10 9 8 7 6 5 4 3 2 1

Library of Congress Cataloging-in-Publication Data
can be found at http://catalog.loc.gov/.

ISBN 978-1-61117-974-3 (hardback)
ISBN 978-1-61117-975-0 (paperback)
ISBN 978-1-61117-976-7 (ebook)

To Steve,
my fellow adventurer

CONTENTS

I

Traveling through Time

It's just so hard to keep a good secret. It consumes your thoughts and haunts your dreams, fighting to make itself known to the world. Sure, a lame secret may be forgotten. But if it's worth knowing at all—like the kind Delta discovered—it really just wants to escape to freedom. That's why the island deserves a lot of credit for keeping its secrets hidden for such a terribly long time. Everything started to unravel, though, on that June afternoon in Pops' office at the museum.

"Close your eyes and hold out your hand."

Twelve-year-old Delta Wells didn't even hesitate as she squeezed her eyes shut and thrust out her open palm. Her summer visits to Hilton Head Island always began like this. Her grandfather would have some little treasure for her that he'd found during the year. It might be a colorful seashell or a sparkly stone or a soft feather from a laughing gull. She kept all of these gifts in a box at home in Chicago, a reminder that Pops thought of her all year long even though they lived a thousand miles apart.

This year's gift felt heavy in her hand. Keeping her eyes closed, she gently jostled the mysterious item, getting a feel for its shape and size. She tightened her fingers around it and felt a thrill as the realization hit her.

"No way, Pops!" she said as her eyes opened wide. "Where'd you get it?"

"Found it on the beach over on the north side of the island," he said, smiling. "I went out right after a big thunder-boomer."

Delta nodded. She knew from all her summers on the South Carolina sea island that the very best time to find treasures on the shore was when a storm had stirred up major waves.

She held the petrified shark tooth up to the desk lamp and examined it more closely. It was the biggest one she'd ever seen, except in books—nearly the size of her palm. The porous bone at the top was deep gray, while the triangular tooth below was shiny and black. Two smaller tri-angles jutted out on either side of the larger one, as if that one sharp blade wouldn't have done enough damage on its own.

"How old do you suppose it is?" Delta asked.

"Oh, I'd say 70 million years or so, when sharks were a lot bigger than they are today."

Pops pushed his glasses up on his nose and leaned over to get a closer look at the prehistoric fossil.

"So this shark was swimming around in the ocean while T-rexes were alive!" Delta said.

She spun around and threw her arms around her grandfather's waist.

"I love it, Pops! It's the best treasure yet!"

Pops patted Delta on the back and kissed the top of her head.

"Thought you'd like it," he said.

Still eyeing the giant tooth in her hand, Delta followed her grandfather out into the display area of the Island History Museum. He and Tootsie, Delta's grandmother, used to just spend their summers on the island when he was a history professor at the University of South Carolina. They had moved to Hilton Head year-round after Pops retired ten years ago. Tootsie always said that her husband wasn't any good at being retired, though, so within a year of leaving teaching, he had taken over the history museum and made it his new career.

"So, have you been anytime interesting lately?" Pops asked with a twinkle in his eye.

"Funny you should ask," Delta responded. "I made a quick stop in ancient Rome last week."

"Met with Julius Caesar, did you?" Pops said.

"Of course! I was his guest at the chariot races. The gladiators were especially gruesome that day."

"Hmm," Pops replied seriously. "Did any get eaten by lions?"

"Just two or three."

Delta and Pops both burst out laughing. "Time Machine" was a game they'd been playing together for years, ever since the summer he had read H.G. Wells's book to her about traveling to the past. He claimed that the famous science fiction author was a distant ancestor of their family, but Delta wasn't sure whether that was true or just part of the game. Either way, it was fun to imagine.

The duo's time travel ended abruptly, though, when two men in suits walked through the door.

"Well, hello, Edward," Pops said, extending his right hand to the man with gray hair. "Wasn't expecting to see a member of the museum board today. You remember my granddaughter, Delta. She and her brother, Jackson, just got here today to spend the summer with us on the island."

Delta put up her hand in a timid wave and the man nodded at her without a smile.

"Could we speak to you . . . privately?" he said to the girl's grandfather.

Delta could take a hint. She wandered over to the "Hands-on Nature" table as Edward introduced Pops to the younger man. She busied herself straightening the samples of various seashells on display on the table, but didn't pay much attention to the men's conversation until she heard the tone of her grandfather's usually-friendly voice harden.

"Well, we haven't gotten the crowds in here that we'd like," Pops said sternly, "but the season's just started."

"Face it," Edward said. "Folks come to Hilton Head for the beaches, the golf, the tennis, the biking. They do not come to an island resort to spend their time in a history museum."

Delta glanced over at the men and then around at the otherwise visitor-free room. The parking lot had been nearly empty when Tootsie dropped them off earlier, too. The museum clearly was not a hot spot on the island.

"The Board of Directors believes we should at least consider Mr. Blakemore's offer to purchase the property," Edward added.

Mr. Blakemore chimed in.

"Just imagine this beautiful site enhanced with condo rentals and twenty-seven holes of golf. Wouldn't that be a better use of this land?"

Delta saw that Pops' face was getting red and his jaw had begun to twitch.

"Delta-boo," he said. "Why don't you head outside and check on your brother."

Delta nodded and headed toward the door, her stomach tightening. She had a feeling her happy summer on the island was about to come to a screeching halt before it had barely begun.

* * * *

The smell hit her as soon as she stepped outside on the museum's front porch.

Delta recognized the earthy tang of lowcountry pluff mud, all sweet grass and salty sea. It was a strange mixture of life and death, with the slick mud's decaying plants and sea life providing nourishment for the living marsh grasses and oyster beds above. To Delta, it was the scent of South

Carolina, of the sea islands, and of visits with Tootsie and Pops. Delta loved that smell.

She plopped down into one of the empty rocking chairs lined up in the shade of the deep front porch. Pops had explained to the kids a hundred times how the museum property used to be a rice plantation way back before the Civil War. After the Union Army took over the island, though, all the Southern plantation owners on Hilton Head had abandoned their slaves and their businesses. This particular plantation had just become a regular farm, and then just a piece of land with an old house on it. But Pops had helped form a Board of Directors that bought the property and turned the old plantation house into a museum to tell the history of the island.

Delta looked out over the broad lawn in front of the building. Huge live oak trees lined both sides of the oyster-shell drive that curved into the distance toward the main road. Filtered sunlight projected moving patterns on the ground beneath the tunnel of ancient trees, with Spanish moss hanging from their branches like Christmas tinsel. Here and there, the open lawn was dotted with the island's native palmetto trees, along with crepe myrtles in full bloom—pinks and purples and reds.

This land belonged to Pops' Island History Museum. Delta scowled as she pictured it replaced with condos and a golf course. Despite what Mr. Blakemore had said, that image was definitely *not* an improvement. Especially if it meant no museum for Pops to run. As long as Delta could remember, visiting her grandparents on the island meant *this* place, just as it was. And what would Pops do without it?

Beyond the trees, past the empty parking lot, was the source of the pluff mud smell. The tidal flats of Broad Creek bordered the museum property, allowing access for fishing and boating in the brackish waters that led out to the Atlantic Ocean. Since Delta couldn't make out any of the heated conversation going on inside the building (she had tried but only heard raised voices), she figured she may as well stroll down to the marshy creek. And anyway, knowing Pops was upset made her feel like a rock was sitting in her stomach. She needed to move.

Delta stepped off the porch of the old plantation house and headed down a path marked by two worn tire tracks in the grass. Not far down the path, she turned past a rack full of kayaks near a clump of trees and found Broad Creek spread out in front of her in all its glory. The water was so wide it didn't look like a creek at all—more like a river or lake. Delta could see across to the other side but the trees over there were tiny and the houses looked like something from a Monopoly game. On both banks of the creek, and even on patches in the middle, tidal grasses swayed in the hot air. Tall marsh birds stood here and there, spreading their wings to the clear summer afternoon as they soaked up the sun's heat.

Delta inhaled deeply. Broad Creek emptied into the ocean at low tide, and then filled with salty water twice daily when the tide rose. She could detect salt and a slightly fishy smell in the air. The tide was heading out now, but much of the mud along the bank was still hidden beneath a foot or more of dark water. In an hour or so, she knew, the oyster beds and pluff mud would be revealed, intensifying that old familiar aroma.

She held her hand across her brow to shield her eyes from the bright afternoon sunlight. What was that moving out in the middle of the creek? She squinted into the sun, and then two thoughts hit her at once. Number one: Pops had told her to go check on her brother. Number two: that was her stupid ten-year-old brother out there alone in a kayak.

"Jax, you idiot!" Delta called. "You know you're not allowed out there by yourself!"

No response.

"If you don't get back here right now, I'm telling!"

But then she remembered Edward and Mr. Blakemore and the way Pops' face had gotten all bright red and his voice had turned to a strange, angry tone that gave Delta that rock in the pit of her stomach. She didn't need to worry her grandfather with anything else right now.

Either Jax was too far away to hear her yelling, or just too stubborn to follow her orders, but one thing was clear. He was *not* steering the kayak back toward shore. Delta was going to have to go out there and get him herself.

2

Diving Right In

Since the water was still relatively close to the high tide line, Delta was able to slide one of the hard plastic kayaks from the rack into the water and step into it without having to get too far out into the muck. Even so, the soles of her tennis shoes got muddy as she climbed into the kayak.

She paddled out into the marsh, following a path between swaying patches of tall grasses poking up through the rippling water. Movement overhead caught her eye and she looked up to see a flock of pelicans fly by in a "V" pattern, searching for a meal.

As she neared her brother, Delta began shouting again.

"Jax! Get your butt over here!"

He heard her this time, and waved happily.

Delta pulled her kayak within a few yards of his.

"Are you crazy? Pops would kill you if he knew you came out here by yourself!"

Jax just shrugged.

"I earned my Kayaking Badge at Boy Scout camp last week. Pops would let me."

"He would not! Not by yourself, and not without a life jacket!" Delta shouted. "What if you had fallen in the creek?"

"I got my Swimming Badge, too. I'd just swim to shore," Jax said. "And anyway, you're out here without a life jacket, too."

Delta groaned.

"Yeah, well, I didn't have a choice! There weren't any jackets by the kayaks, but I had to come out here anyway to get your sorry butt," she said. "They should have given you the Moron Badge."

"Well, then you should get the Fun-Sucker Badge because you suck the fun out of everything," Jax responded.

Delta let that one pass.

"What were you doing out here anyway?" she asked.

"I had to come," Jax said. "I think I saw a shark."

"What?"

"I saw a fin and so I had to come see if it was a shark."

"Jax, sharks don't come all the way back here in the creek," Delta said. "And even if you *did* see one, what the heck were you going to do if you got close to it?"

"Smack it in the nose with my paddle," he responded. "I heard that makes them go away."

Delta groaned louder.

"Jax, you make absolutely no sense! Why not just leave the poor thing alone!"

Just then, a fin broke the surface of the water not far from the kayaks.

"There it is! I told you!" Jax shouted, pointing.

A gray back arched out of the water, and the siblings watched silently as the animal submerged and reappeared, leaping completely into the air before splashing back into Broad Creek.

"It was a dolphin, you doofus!" Delta said with a laugh.

Jax just smiled sheepishly.

"Well, I guess it's a good thing I didn't hit it with my paddle," he said.

* * * *

With his "shark" encounter completed, Jax put up no fight following his sister back toward the museum property. As the two kayaks approached the shore, though, Delta noticed that the tide had moved out a lot while they had been out on the creek. About a hundred feet of pluff mud was now exposed between the water's edge and the dry land. Unless Delta found a deeper channel to shore, she and her brother would have to trudge through that sticky muck to drag the kayaks back to the bank.

Delta peered up and down the shoreline until she found a nearby spot that seemed to have water extending nearly to dry land.

"Hey, Jax," she called, pointing to the preferred docking site. "Let's head over there. We can paddle almost all the way to shore."

It was a fine plan, but, as usual, Jax didn't listen and just jumped right overboard then and there. He landed with a SCHLOOP and immediately sunk up to his knees in the mud.

"Jax, I told you to go ashore over here!" Delta yelled.

"I'm fine," Jax said, trying to pull his legs from the mire.

He had to lift each foot high to clear the surface, and then swing his leg forward awkwardly with each step, dragging his kayak through the mud behind him.

From her own boat, still bobbing in the shallow water, Delta rolled her eyes and laughed.

By the time Jax finally reached shore, he was covered up to his hips in mud. As he tried to stomp some of the excess goop off his feet, Delta noticed something strange.

"Where's your other shoe?" she called to her brother.

Jax looked down at his feet.

"Oops!" he said.

Apparently, the pluff mud had sucked one of his shoes off and the little goofwad had just left it out there.

"It's probably in one of those foot-holes," Jax yelled. "See if you can find it!"

Leg-size holes in the mud led a direct path to shore.

Great, Delta thought. *He does something stupid and I have to fix it.*

"Which hole?" Delta shouted back.

Jax shrugged.

"Well, how long was the shoe off your foot?" she asked. "Did it come off as soon as you got out of the kayak, or not until you were closer to shore?"

"I didn't know it was off at all until you said something," Jax replied.

Delta groaned.

How could he lose the shoe right off his foot and not even notice it?

She used the paddle to pull her kayak toward the nearest leg hole. She could reach in and grab the shoe when she found it.

When she got to the hole and looked down, though, she realized it was a couple of feet deep and starting to pool with water. She couldn't see whether the shoe was in there or not.

She leaned over the edge of the kayak, sticking her arm into the muddy hole. But before her finger tips reached the bottom, the kayak flipped and she landed—SPLAT—in the pluff mud.

She could hear Jax laughing hysterically.

As she rolled around trying to right herself, Delta managed to completely cover herself in muck. She reached back down into the leg hole and, wouldn't you know it, there was no shoe. She trudged to the next one, and the next, before she finally felt something solid at the bottom of a soppy hole.

"Found it," she shouted toward shore. "You owe me so big, Jax!"

She hooked her fingers into the foot opening of the shoe and had to give it a hard tug to pull it free from the sticky mud.

But it was not a shoe. Not at all.

Delta's hand was stuffed inside the mouth of a human skull.

Holding the Head

Delta screamed when she saw the skull's teeth clenching her hand. A tingle began in her fingers and grew into a jolt of electricity by the time it reached her shoulder. Flinging her find back into the hole, she tried to run from the spot, but the pluff mud slowed her efforts.

"Delta? What *was* that?" Jax yelled from shore.

"Ooh, ooh, ooh!" Delta flailed the hand that had touched the muddy bone, as if she could remove the memory of it.

"It looked like a *skull!*" her brother said, wide-eyed.

"It *was* a skull! A *human* one!" Delta's heart was racing.

"Awesome!" Jax shouted, and starting trudging back through the marsh toward her.

The boy reached into the hole and pulled the skull back out. As he turned it over in his hand, muddy water poured out of it like a pitcher pouring chocolate milk.

Delta flinched as the reality of the situation began to sink in. It had been bad enough thinking she was sticking her fingers in Jax's gross shoe, but she had actually stuck her hand inside somebody's head!

"This is so cool!" Jax said.

Delta watched as her brother, still holding the skull, stuck his other arm into the hole. After wiggling it around for a minute or so, he pulled his arm back out and held a long bone.

"Ta-da!" he shouted triumphantly.

Just then, a deep voice called across the water.

"What in blazes are you kids doing out there?" Pops yelled.

"We found a skeleton, Pops!" Jax responded. "A skeleton of a *person!*"

The boy proudly raised the bones so his grandfather could see them.

After only a moment's hesitation, Pops said, "Put them back where you found them, Jackson, but mark the spot."

"But, Pops!" Jax cried, "I wanted to keep them!"

"I'm calling 911," Pops replied. "The sheriff should be the one doing the digging."

Glancing around her, Delta reached for a nearby reed and yanked it out of the muck by the roots. She stuck it like a flag in the hole where the bones had been buried, and motioned to her brother to dispose of them. With a heavy sigh, he dropped the skull and longer bone into the water with a splash.

The kids made their way out of the marsh, with Delta dragging her kayak behind her. As they stepped from the thick pluff mud onto dry shoreline, they heard Pops explaining over the phone that he needed to report a human skeleton discovered near the Island History Museum.

"Did you hear that, Delta?" Jax said, grinning from ear to ear. "We made a 'discovery'! We'll be famous!"

"Shut up, Jax," Delta said. "You know, if you'd kept your shoe on I would never have found that thing!"

"You're welcome!" he said.

Delta groaned and rolled her eyes.

How could he think this was a *good* thing? That skeleton used to be somebody, after all. *Inside* somebody.

"Do you think a whole skeleton is out there?" Jax asked. "Like arms and legs and feet and everything?"

His excitement made Delta want to punch him.

"Well, the sheriff should be here shortly," Pops said, putting his phone back in his pocket. "Are you kids alright?"

"I'm great!" Jax said.

"Oh, no!" Delta cried. "My phone was in my pocket!"

She pulled out the new smart phone she had begged her parents to get her before this trip and found it soaked with mud and briny water. Delta tried in vain to turn it on, but the dark screen just lay there, as if mocking her.

She looked up and saw her grandfather's concerned face. The stress from the museum trouble was already worrying him, and now this skeleton mess.

She shrugged and stuck the ruined phone back in her pocket.

"No big deal," she lied. "I was going to get a new one soon, anyway."

She couldn't risk adding to Pops' stress any more than she already had. After all, how much more worry could he take?

II

Dealing with Questions

The Beaufort County Sheriff's Department didn't get a lot of action, so it took them less than ten minutes to get to the tidal flats. A local newspaper reporter, apparently tipped off by a contact in the department, was there in less than fifteen. Delta had never been interviewed by a law enforcement officer—or a reporter, for that matter. Pops said to just tell them what she knew, so that's what she did. She didn't know much, though, except that having all these extra people around made this strange situation downright surreal.

"Darlin', how did you happen to find that skeleton?" a reporter who introduced herself as "Miss Barbara" asked.

Delta told her, step by step, about kayaking and Jax's lost shoe and tipping over into the pluff mud. Miss Barbara laughed in all the right places and wrote with a pen in a spiral notebook.

"But now, what about that skeleton?" the reporter asked.

"Well, I found the skull, but my brother found the other bone," Delta said.

She left out the part about screaming and throwing the skull back into the marsh.

After Miss Barbara had asked all her questions, a photographer wanted to take a picture of Delta and Jax and Pops for the newspaper. It would be pretty cool to be in the paper, she guessed, but Delta sure wished she wasn't covered in muck. She tried to smooth her hair down and wipe some of the mud off with her hand, but that didn't improve things much. She smiled as best she could for the picture and hoped no one would notice how dirty she was.

When Delta finished dealing with the press, she turned her attention to the progress being made by the Sheriff's Department.

Digging with shovels, the deputies had already found several more bones, including a length of spine and some ribs. Officers in galoshes were sticking big plastic panels in the muck, blocking off a wide area around the spot where Delta had found the skull. Pops said the panels would help keep some of the water out when the tide came back in so the deputies could search the area. When they got the barricades in place, one of them strung yellow tape all around the sides of it.

Caked in dried mud, Delta and Jax stood on the grass under a live oak tree.

"Whose skeleton do you think it is?" Jax asked.

"How should I know?" Delta said.

"What if it was a murder!"

Delta didn't want to encourage her brother, but she wondered about that, too. The sheriff must think it was a possibility. After all, the yellow tape said "Crime Scene" all over it. But Hilton Head Island just wasn't a place where murders happened.

Was it?

"Who do you think did it?" Jax asked.

"We don't know that anyone did it," Delta said.

"Maybe we'll get a big reward!"

"They don't give rewards for finding bodies, Jax."

"Well, maybe we'll be famous!"

"Just shut up," his sister replied, looking out toward the water.

Pops stood by the shoreline having a serious conversation with the sheriff. They had been friends for years, just from living on the island. Delta figured this was probably the first time they'd spoken in an official "police business" sort of way, though.

She looked past Pops and saw that a couple of deputies were inside the boundaries of the barricade. Delta saw one place more bones in a big plastic bag and hand it to another deputy waiting in the marsh. He trudged to shore and placed the bag in the trunk of one of the cruisers.

Delta watched the man slam the trunk lid and head back out into the mud with a new, empty plastic bag, stepping carefully in his knee-high galoshes.

When he got back out to the barricade, the deputy nearly bumped into a boy standing nearby. Dressed in gray pants and shirt, the boy looked to be about Delta's age.

What's he doing out there? Delta wondered.

Jax was apparently thinking the same thing.

"That kid's not supposed to be out there by the crime scene," he said. "They wouldn't let us stay out there and we found the skeleton. It's not fair for him to be out there watching if we can't."

"Maybe his dad is one of the officers or something," Delta said.

She watched the boy to see if anyone would tell him to move, but no one did.

When Pops finished talking to the sheriff, he joined his grandchildren under the live oak tree.

"Well, kiddos, let's get you home and hose you off," he said. "Tootsie's not going to believe I let you get so dirty."

"Is the sheriff through with us?" Delta asked.

"Yes, we've done our part," Pops replied. "We ought to get out of their way and let them do their jobs."

"But he's not out of their way," Jax said.

"Who's not?" Pops asked.

"The kid that's been hanging out by the 'crime scene' tape," said Jax. "How come they let him stand so close?"

"What kid?" Pops asked, looking toward the water.

Delta followed his gaze and saw the tape and the sheriff's deputies. But the boy in gray was gone. She glanced around the tidal flats, but did not see him anywhere. Maybe the deputies had finally told him to leave.

Pops led the way back up the path to the museum's parking lot.

"Why don't you kiddos ride in back," Pops said. "Won't that be fun?"

Delta knew Pops just didn't want them getting the inside of his truck dirty, but that was alright. She didn't mind riding in the truck bed. Between the threat of the museum closing, and then this craziness in the marsh, this afternoon had been so unreal that it left her feeling kind of numb. It would feel good to ride down familiar roads, past familiar sights. Maybe the wind blowing in her face as they rode would wake her up from this strange dream and she'd discover that it never really happened at all.

Pops boosted Delta and Jax into the back of the truck and climbed into the cab.

Bouncing over the gravel road that led away from the museum, Delta felt the rush of warm wind hit her and she sighed.

What a weird, weird day.

Suddenly, Jax started waving his arms and shouting.

"Travis! Hey, Travis! Guess what we found!"

Delta glanced across the museum lawn and saw a teenager on a riding mower in the distance. Hopefully the noise from the machine would drown Jax out.

Delta threw one arm around her brother's shoulders and clamped the other hand over his mouth, pulling him down into the bed of the truck.

"Shut up, Jax!" she said through clenched teeth.

Delta thought back to her first meeting with Travis earlier that day, when Tootsie had dropped the kids off at the museum. While Pops was greeting the rest of the family on the front porch, a boy a few years older than Delta had approached the group.

"How're you doing there, Travis?" Pops had asked cheerfully.

The teen was wearing an "Island History Museum" T-shirt and khaki shorts, and held a rake in his hand. His blond hair curled around his ears, and Delta could still picture him running his hand through it to sweep the hair from his eyes.

"Pretty good, sir," Travis had replied. "I finished spreading that mulch and was about to head home for a late lunch, if that's alright." His Southern accent added to his charm.

He had glanced over at Delta then.

"Hey," he said, smiling.

"Travis, I'd like you to meet my grandkids—Delta, and this is Jackson." Pops was the only person who ever called Jax by his whole name. Except maybe for Mom when she was mad.

"You can call me Jax," the younger boy had quickly corrected.

"Hey." Travis tipped his chin to Jax.

"So you work here at the museum?"

Delta couldn't believe she had said something so stupid! Of course he worked at the museum. *ARGH!*

"Yeah, just for the summer," he said. "I go to boarding school in Charleston during the school year."

He had pronounced it like "Chahl-ston."

"Yeah, I go to school in Chicago," Delta said. "I live there, actually."

"Cool."

A few beats had passed with no conversation, and then Travis stuck out his hand to Pops, who shook it.

"See you later, sir," Travis said, and then he turned and smiled at Delta.

"See ya around," he said.

Delta had smiled, too, as she watched him walk away.

See ya around!

Now, pinning her little brother to the floor of the pickup truck, Delta smiled again at the memory. She did hope to see Travis again this summer, but the last thing she needed was for him to see her at this moment all covered in marsh mud!

As she bent her arm and noticed the drying mud crack with her movement, Delta's thoughts returned to the more pressing issues at hand. Whose skeleton had they discovered this afternoon, and what was it doing hiding in the pluff mud of Broad Creek?

Finding a Gift

Delta awoke the next morning to voices coming from down the hall. She dragged herself from bed and wandered into the kitchen, where Jax was listening to Tootsie read aloud from the morning newspaper.

". . . initial examinations indicate that the remains are not recent, but rather appear to be more than 100 years old."

"Wow!" Jax said, munching on a bowl of cereal.

"Isn't that something?" Tootsie said. "Y'all dug up some Hilton Head history!"

"It was still a person," Delta added, dropping into a chair at the table.

"Well, of course it was, sweetie!" Tootsie hugged her granddaughter's shoulders from behind.

"I know it must have been pretty traumatic for you finding it and all, but there is some peace of mind knowing that whatever happened to that poor soul happened a long time ago. There's no family out there right now looking for a missing loved one."

"Or a crazy murderer wandering the island," Jax said.

He sounded almost disappointed.

Delta shrugged.

"I guess."

Tootsie scanned the rest of the article.

"It says the sheriff's office is going to transfer the remains to the State Archaeological Museum in Charleston since it's not really a criminal investigation."

Tootsie looked up from the paper.

"Your grandfather knows some folks who work over there, so we'll have to be sure and get the scoop on what they figure out."

"Show her the pictures!" Jax said.

Tootsie spread the newspaper on the table and right there on the front page was a huge picture of Delta, Jax, and Pops in all their muddy glory. Next to it, another photo showed a bunch of bones, including the skull. Delta shuddered, remembering the jolt it had given her touching that thing.

"Looks like y'all are island celebrities!" Tootsie said.

* * * *

Jax took forever picking a new pair of tennis shoes at the sporting goods store. Tootsie was way more patient with him than Mom would have been, letting him try on like a dozen styles—all more expensive than Mom would have paid, too. Delta sat slumped in a vinyl-clad chair, sighing loudly every few minutes. When her brother finally selected a pair, he kept them on and stuffed his flip flops in a bag that a guy at the check-out counter gave Tootsie when she paid.

"How about stopping by to visit Pops?" Tootsie said as they climbed into her lime green Volkswagen Beetle.

With its curvy shape and the fresh flowers that were always in the dashboard vase, the Bug was a fun car. Tootsie always liked to ride with the top down, because she said the wind blowing through her short, spiky hairdo was like a free stylist. Delta liked the car well enough, but she hated how Jax always punched her arm and yelled, "Slug bug!" every time they saw it.

Delta instinctively covered her arm with her hand as they approached the car, but this time her brother was distracted by other thoughts.

"Great idea, Tootsie!" he said. "We can show you where we found the skeleton!"

There were so many cars at the museum that Tootsie had to park in the third row of spaces, but there were practically no visitors inside when they entered the building.

"Where is everybody?" Tootsie asked Pops when they found him in his office. "I haven't seen the parking lot this full for ages!"

"They're all checking out the burial site," Pops replied. "There's a whole crowd of folks over by the marsh. Y'all should go over there so they can meet the famous discoverers!"

He winked at Delta and Jax.

"Wow! It didn't take long for the news to get out!" Jax said.

Tootsie laughed.

"Well, we don't get much news like this on Hilton Head, so it's a big deal!" she said.

Delta jumped when a gruff voice behind her spoke.

"Somebody parked in my begonias."

The speaker reminded Delta of the kind of men who hung out under the overpasses in downtown Chicago. He looked ancient, with a scraggly grey beard and mustache, watery blue eyes, and dirt on one cheek. He wore baggy black pants and a T-shirt that looked like they hadn't been washed in weeks. Smelled like it, too. Delta cringed and unconsciously stepped away.

"I guess that's a good problem to have," Pops told the man. "In a couple of days, the novelty will wear off and we'll wish we had people parking all over the place."

The old man grunted and turned to leave. As he did, Delta noticed with a start that, while his right hand was crusted in dirt and grime, where his left hand should have been she saw only a glint of silver. He was gone before she could get a better look.

"Who was that?" Jax asked, wide-eyed.

"Captain DeFoe," Pops replied, tapping the corner of a framed photo on his desk. The picture showed a group of people all dressed in shirts with the Island History Museum logo on the front. They were standing on the front steps of the building.

Probably the people who work here, Delta thought.

Pops had pointed to a cleaner, better groomed version of the man who had just left his office. Curiously, the man in the photo had a parrot perched on his shoulder.

"He's in charge of the building and grounds," Pops said.

"Is he always such a grouch?" Jax asked.

Pops sighed.

"He's having a tough time of it, is all. Best stay out of his way, kiddos."

No problem there!

Delta had no intention of going anywhere near that sketchy old man.

"Why don't we let Pops get back to work and y'all show me where you made your big discovery yesterday?" Tootsie said, leading the way out of Pops' office.

The trio hiked up the path toward the marsh, hearing voices in the distance. When they arrived at the spot where they'd parked the truck the previous day, they were met by at least twenty spectators. Some talked excitedly, while others pointed toward the spot in the water where bright yellow tape and plastic barricades marked the location where Delta had placed her hand inside the skeleton's head.

One of the visitors recognized Tootsie and waved her over.

"My goodness!" the woman said. "You invite your grandkids to the island and look what excitement they churn up!"

The woman laughed heartily, her dark curls bouncing in the sunlight. Tootsie put her arm across her friend's back and shared the laugh.

"Well, aren't I always bragging about how amazing they are?"

More spectators joined the women and chatted, until Jax, hungry for attention, wiggled conspicuously into the group.

"Here's one of our little heroes now!" Tootsie said, adding, "Get on over here, Delta, so I can show you off to my friends!"

Delta trudged over to her grandmother and smiled weakly as the group of islanders made a fuss over the two kids. As it became apparent to everyone near the marsh that these were the pair from the newspaper photo, the kids were barraged with questions about their discovery. A couple of people even took selfies with Delta and Jax, which Jax loved and Delta did not.

Eventually, after they had answered everyone's questions and posed for everyone's photos, Delta and her brother sat in the shade of a tree while their grandmother continued visiting with the assembled group.

"Hey, look who's here again," Jax said, motioning toward a lone figure standing on the edge of the marsh.

The kid was a ways down the bank from where everyone else was hanging out, but even from a distance Delta recognized it was the same guy from the "crime scene" last night.

"I'm gonna ask him what his deal is," Jax said, heading toward the boy.

Delta followed, eyeing the kid curiously. It looked like he was still wearing the same clothes from before, but as they got nearer she could see that they were baggy on him and his shirt had patches sewn on here and there. Delta didn't know any really poor kids, or at least she didn't think she did. She knew there were kids at her school who got free lunches, but it was all done in secret so she didn't know specifically who those kids were. From the way he was dressed, this kid probably qualified for free lunch at his school.

The boy was staring intently into the grassy water and didn't even seem to notice them at first as they approached him.

"Hi," Jax said, but got no response.

"Hey, weren't you here last night when they were digging up that skeleton?" he added.

When the kid still didn't answer, Jax said, "You know, we were the ones that discovered the bones."

With that news, the boy finally looked up and Delta saw his face close up for the first time. His hair was brown and shaggy, and his eyes were dark and serious. He stared right at her without a hint of a friendly smile, and then shifted his gaze back to the water.

"What's your name?" Jax tried, but still got no response.

Awkward.

It was obvious the kid did not want to talk to them.

"Come on, Jax," Delta said, pulling at her brother's arm.

"Whatever," he shrugged, and headed back toward Tootsie and the rest of the sightseers.

Delta followed slowly behind him. Something about that boy made her feel sad. Not his hand-me-down clothes or his unkempt hair. It was the look in his eyes. He seemed way too serious for a kid their age.

She glanced back over her shoulder and caught the boy looking at her, too. She smiled at him and he nodded in reply, but still no smile.

When they reached Tootsie, she was bragging to some more onlookers about how her family had made "the big discovery."

"Here are the stars of the hour!" she said, putting an arm around each of them.

"How exciting!" a man in denim shorts and a Hilton Head T-shirt said. "I'll bet you didn't expect to spend your vacation finding buried treasure!"

Delta grunted and rolled her eyes.

Some treasure!

As the kids headed toward the parked Bug with Tootsie, Jax spoke up.

"I was just trying to be friendly, you know. That kid didn't have to be so rude."

"What kid?" Tootsie asked.

"The one with patched clothes from last night. He was here again today, but when I tried to talk to him he wouldn't even answer."

Tootsie looked in the direction Jax had motioned, but as they followed her gaze they saw that he was no longer there.

"Hm," Tootsie said. "I guess I didn't see him."

"How could you not see him, Tootsie!" Jax said.

He walked back toward the spot where they had spoken to the boy.

"He was standing here for like fifteen minutes just staring into the water like a weirdo."

Jax reenacted the boy's stance, standing at the shoreline gazing into the marsh.

"Maybe he's disabled or something, Jax," Delta said, feeling protective of the boy. "You don't know what his story is so you shouldn't just assume he's rude or weird."

But Jax wasn't even listening to his sister.

"Hey, look what I found!" he shouted, pointing into a patch of marsh grass.

"Jax! Your new shoes!" Tootsie groaned, but it was too late.

Jax tromped a few feet through the pluff mud and stuck his arm into the water. After twisting it around for a few seconds, he raised it triumphantly.

"See!"

Jax held an old brown bottle in his fist. About the size of the wine bottles Delta had seen at restaurants, this one had aged until its glass was frosty rather than clear.

"I'll bet this is what the kid was looking at in the water, but I got it!" Jax said. "Sorry, Patchy! You snooze, you lose!"

"It's just an old bottle, Jax," Delta said.

"Not *just* an old bottle," her brother said. "Pops loves old stuff like this. I can give it to him for his birthday in a few weeks."

Delta figured that did make sense. Pops probably would think it was cool. She kind of felt bad for Patchy, though, since he had apparently seen it first.

Jax trudged back to shore and Tootsie made him take off his new muddy shoes.

At least he didn't leave one behind in the pluff mud this time!

"Slip your flip-flops back on and let's get these shoes home and throw them in the washer," Tootsie said with a sigh.

As they climbed into the Bug and headed toward home, Delta glanced back toward the tidal flats. The crowd had dispersed and it looked quiet again. Sunlight glistened on the water and she saw a pair of dolphins leap about halfway across the creek. If it weren't for the bright yellow tape still staked out in the marsh, you'd never know this place was anything but peaceful.

Even in the heat, Delta felt a chill run down her spine.

Something awful had happened in that marsh, but would she ever know what it was? Would she rather not know at all?

6

Breaking the News

Pops was late getting home that evening, and he was not a happy camper.

"Damn that City Council!" he said, slamming a leather folder on the kitchen counter.

Delta had never heard him curse before. His face was bright red and she wondered if getting so angry could give a man his age a heart attack. Just the thought put a big lump in her stomach.

"No luck?" Tootsie asked quietly, leading him toward the den with a nod toward the kids.

Delta had seen her own parents use that tactic enough times. She knew it meant the adults wanted to speak privately, but that usually meant whatever they were talking about was super important. She tiptoed down the hallway and leaned against the wall just within earshot.

"They're a bunch of short-sighted fools!" she heard Pops say in a loud whisper. "Can't find a penny in the budget for the museum, but they're sponsoring some idiotic cardboard boat race over on Skull Creek."

Delta didn't say so, but she thought that boat race sounded kind of interesting.

"Well, then, we'll just think of something else. No point getting bogged down by 'noes' when there's got to be some 'yeses' out there somewhere!"

Good old Tootsie. Always thinking on the bright side.

"I'm still hoping for some money from the State Historical Commission," Pops said.

"Well, there you go!" said Tootsie.

Delta hurried back to the kitchen, as if she had been there the whole time. Tootsie walked back into the room, clearly still consumed with thoughts of the museum, and sighed.

"He's devoted the last ten years of his life to that museum," she said, shaking her head. "It'd just *kill* him if it had to close."

Delta hoped Tootsie wasn't going to start crying or something.

Noticing the girl's wide-eyed face, though, Tootsie perked up.

"Oh, sweetie! That's just an expression! Everything will be fine."

She gave Delta a quick hug and then disappeared back down the hall toward the den.

"Jeez! What was *that* all about?" Jax said.

With all the excitement at the marsh, with the skeleton and all, Delta hadn't thought to mention to her brother about the possible sale of the museum property.

"Some bozo real estate developer wants to buy the museum and turn it into a golf resort," she whispered. "I heard them talking yesterday while you were out kayaking."

Jax frowned.

"But Pops would still get to run the museum, right?" he asked. "It would just be part of the resort?"

"No, there wouldn't *be* a museum anymore," Delta said. "They'd probably turn the building into a clubhouse or something."

"But what about all the people who want to come to the museum?" Jax asked.

"That's the problem," she said. "Not many people go, so the Board of Directors thinks they might as well sell it. The museum doesn't make enough money, and they don't think people would miss it if it closed."

"Well, *I* would miss it," Jax said. "And I know Pops would!"

Delta nodded.

"Pops is hoping someone will donate money to help save it."

"I don't have much money," Jax said sadly, "but I would help if I could."

"Yeah, me, too," his sister said.

* * * *

Delta's room for the summer was the spare bedroom that Tootsie used as an art studio. In her "first life" (as Tootsie referred to her pre-retirement years), she had been a real estate agent, but now she called herself "an artiste." Her paintings were wild and colorful, and occasionally she sold one of them at an art gallery on the island.

Against one wall sat a daybed, covered in a poofy down comforter. Tootsie kept a bajillion pillows, all in bright colors and crazy patterns, piled on the bed. Like Pops' den, this room had some shelves, too, but these were filled with art supplies—paints of every color, jars filled with brushes of various sizes, and extra canvases propped here and there.

An easel sat in one corner, near the window, with a half-finished painting propped on it. Splashes of golds and yellows filled the bottom, with slashes of blue across the top half. Greens climbed the sides and hung across the top. Somehow it made Delta think of water and trees.

As she stood staring at the painting, Jax threw the door open and burst into the room.

"Jeez, Jax! Have you heard of knocking?"

"Sorry."

He plopped down on the end of the daybed.

"What's your problem?" Delta asked with a scowl.

"No problem," Jax replied, oblivious to her sarcasm. "I washed Pops' bottle off in the bathroom sink. It looks even cooler now!"

He held up the brown glass bottle, now free of the muck that had previously coated most of it. Delta could only imagine what a mess the bathroom sink must be now.

"Look! It has writing on it!" Jax said.

Delta took the bottle from his hand and held it up to the floor lamp next to her. Sure enough, the bottle had a raised design and lettering. Some type of leaf—a maple leaf, maybe—was centered on the bottle, while the words "Southern Dew" curved around it.

"It must have had soda pop in it," Jax said. "Like Mountain Dew."

Delta smirked.

"Not likely, goofball. It says '90 proof' on it. It was probably some kind of whiskey."

The bottle appeared to be sort of amber in color, although the years in the marsh had aged the glass so that it was entirely opaque. Delta imagined it had once been clear and might have actually been kind of pretty if the light hit it the right way. The bottle felt too light to still be full, but someone had stuck an old cork way down in its neck, too far to pull out.

"Give it," Jax said, reaching for the bottle. "I want to shine it up some more and find a good hiding place for it until Pops' birthday."

Delta pulled the bottle just out of his grasp.

"What'll you give me for it?" she asked.

"Nothing!" Jax responded. "It's mine! Give it back!"

Delta stood up and held her arm up as high as she could. She laughed as her brother leapt for the bottle, knowing that he hadn't had his growth spurt yet and would never be able to reach it.

"Stop it, Delta!" Jax said, still jumping. Delta raised her other arm and began tossing the bottle back and forth between her hands.

"You almost got it!" she teased.

Jax grabbed at Delta's right arm just as she tossed the bottle with her left. They both watched the boy's treasure fall as if in slow motion. Long before it hit the carpeted floor, though, it hit the edge of Tootsie's desk. With a gasp, Delta heard the crack of old glass against wood. The bottle bounced to the carpet in several pieces.

"Oh, no!" Jax already looked near tears.

"I am *so* sorry!" Delta said.

She had only been kidding. She hadn't meant to do any real harm.

Jax was kneeling over the bottle on the floor, quietly picking through chunks of glass.

"Don't cut yourself, Jax!"

That would make Delta feel even worse! She waited for him to start yelling at her, or swatting at her, or *something*. As he started to turn his head toward her, Delta dreaded seeing the hurt look in his eyes.

He was grinning from ear to ear.

7

Getting the Message

"Look what I found!"

Jax was holding what looked like an old rolled-up rag in his hand.

"It was inside the bottle."

He carefully held up his latest find, allowing the cloth to slowly unfurl. The fabric was browned and stained, with frayed edges. It was square-shaped, about six inches across, and on closer inspection it looked to Delta like an old pocket of some kind. As if someone had torn it right off their clothes.

Jax flipped the fabric over and both kids responded in unison.

"Whoa!"

A swirly kind of cursive writing covered the cloth in a dark ink. It was smudged in spots, but apparently the fabric had been thick enough to keep it from bleeding through to the other side. Jax placed the square on Tootsie's desk and Delta pulled the lamp over so they could get a better look.

It took the kids nearly an hour to decipher what the writing said, arguing over many of the words until the message they agreed upon at least made grammatical sense. Even then, though, they had no idea what the words meant.

As far as they could determine, the message on the torn piece of cloth was:

Nov 7 1861
To Col Geo Bingham, Bluffton
Under heavy naval attack
Send assistance
If defeated Jasper's Gems
can be found under the light of
Hilton Head arch
—Col Wm Wagener, Ft Walker

"1861! Man, that's *old!*" Jax said.

"No kidding!" his sister agreed.

"Who do you suppose 'Geo Bingham' and 'Wim Wagener' are?"

"I don't know, but they're not anybody anymore!" Delta said.

She took a closer look at the message.

"'Geo' probably means 'George' and 'Wm' stands for 'William,'" she added.

"Isn't 'Bluffton' that town on the other side of the bridge? Before you get to Hilton Head?" Jax asked.

"That's right," Delta said, impressed that Jax had even noticed what town they drove through coming from the airport.

"What's 'Fut Walker'?"

"'Fort Walker,'" Delta corrected. "And I don't know."

"Let's Google it!"

Sometimes, on rare occasions, Jax actually came up with some pretty good ideas. The computer monitor was right there on Tootsie's desk, hidden behind stacks of art supply catalogs and racks holding various sizes and shapes of paint brushes. The keyboard was shoved between papers on a top shelf. Jax pushed all of the art stuff to the side and Delta flipped the switch on the computer tower underneath the desk. No light came on. There was no humming sound.

"Turn the monitor on," Jax suggested.

Delta pressed the button on the edge of the screen, but the lit monitor glowed a blank gray color.

"Maybe it's not plugged in," Jax said.

Delta checked. It was.

"I'll ask Tootsie for help," she said, heading toward the hallway.

"Don't tell her what we're doing, though!" Jax whispered urgently. "I still want this to be a surprise!"

Delta found her grandmother watching television in the living room.

"Um, Tootsie," she began. "I was wanting to watch some videos on your computer. Is there something special I need to do to get it to work?"

Tootsie looked up and waved her hand dismissively.

"Oh, sweetie, that old thing quit working last winter and I never did get it fixed. I haven't missed it, so I figure I'll just simplify my life by not being computerized!"

"Oh," Delta responded. "Does Pops have a computer I could use?"

"Only at the office, Delta-Boo. Why don't you just watch some TV with me?"

Delta glanced at the screen and saw that Tootsie was watching an old episode of a 1970's television series on the Hallmark Channel.

"Uh, that's okay," she replied. "I guess I'll just turn in for the night."

She headed back to her room and broke the news to Jax.

"No computer. Can you believe it?"

Jax shook his head in shared disbelief.

If only my phone hadn't died in the marsh! Delta thought.

"Maybe we can go to the library or something," Jax said, ever hopeful. "This sounds like clues to a treasure—you know, 'Jasper's Gems'—and I've got to find it for Pops' birthday!"

Delta laughed.

"Yeah, right. Treasure!"

But then she saw the look of disappointment on her little brother's face, and the chunks of broken glass still lying on the carpet. She had ruined Jax's present for their grandfather, and the boy hadn't even gotten mad about it. She guessed she owed him a little something.

"Sure, maybe we can figure out your message," she said with a shrug.

Jax brightened.

"Hey, if we really do find treasure, maybe Pops can use it to save the museum!"

Delta hadn't thought of that. She was 99 percent sure there was no trea-sure to be found, but what about that other 1 percent? Could this message be the answer to Pops' problems?

Seeing the Sound

Tootsie was helping organize an upcoming art fair on the island, so she spent the next couple of days in what she called "planning mode" and couldn't drive the kids to the library.

"Check your phone," Jax told his sister. "Maybe it's working again, and we can use the wi-fi to google the message."

Delta had heard somewhere that putting a wet cell phone in a bag of uncooked rice would dry it out, so it had been sealed up for several days now.

Standing in her room, the girl's heart pounded as she unzipped the plastic bag. If this hadn't worked, her new phone was dead for good.

Jax strained to get a better look, practically sticking his head in the bag.

"Scoot back, Jax!" she said with a shove.

Delta carefully lifted the phone and turned it over in her hand to ex-amine it. It *looked* dry enough. She pulled the battery out of the rice, too, and put it back in its place. She took a deep breath and looked up at her brother.

"Well, I guess it's now or never."

The kids' heads bumped as they both leaned over the screen, but neither noticed. Delta pushed the power button and . . . .

Nothing happened.

"Maybe you didn't push it right," Jax said, jerking the phone from his sister's hand.

"I know how to turn on my own cell phone!" Delta said, retrieving it. "It's just dead! I've killed it!"

Delta plopped down hard on the daybed. She had sworn to her parents that she was responsible enough to take care of the expensive electronic device, and now she had gone and ruined it on the first day she got to the island! It would take a lot of begging to get them to replace it for her. She'd probably have to spend the rest of the summer without a phone at all!

Delta's pity-party ended abruptly when she heard Pops walk in the door from work. She peeked down the hallway and noticed that he had dark circles under his eyes and somehow looked older than he had just a few days ago.

He walked into the living room with a heavy sigh and sank into an armchair.

"How was your day?" Delta heard Tootsie ask tentatively.

"The developers had surveyors out at the museum," he said. "They're already planning their golf resort and the sale isn't even finalized yet!"

Tootsie was standing next to Pops' chair, with her arm draped protectively around his neck. She looked nearly as sad and worn out as he did.

"Is there anything more you can do about it at this point?" she asked her husband.

"Well, I'm still holding out hope for money from the State Historical Commission," he said.

When Tootsie looked up and saw the kids standing in the entrance to the living room, she put on a smile that other people might think was real, but that Delta could tell was a fake.

"I know what we should do tonight!" Tootsie said. "Let's go out for a nice dinner! Won't that be fun?"

Delta wasn't really in the mood for fun, and she suspected that Pops wasn't either. In any case, though, Tootsie had made no preparations for cooking dinner, so eating out was as good a plan as any.

* * * *

The restaurant Pops chose was located across the island, facing Port Royal Sound. Delta stared out the car window as the family headed out of her grandparents' neighborhood. Like much of Hilton Head Island, Palmetto Dunes Plantation was located on the site of an old pre-Civil-War farm. Now each of the former plantations was a neighborhood with homes, pools, tennis courts, shops, and restaurants—all just a short walk or bike ride to the beach. Palmetto Dunes was filled with beautifully landscaped tropical plants, and was laced with sparkling freshwater canals, one of which ran right past Pops' backyard.

As they drove past a lake surrounded by palmetto trees, she spotted an official sign by the side of the road—"Do Not Feed Alligators." Gators were everywhere down here. It was common to see them lounging in the grass near a pond, or sometimes swimming across the surface of the water. In previous summers, Delta and Jax had made a game of counting how many gators they could spot during a visit. A couple of years ago, they saw 34 in just two weeks.

"Hey, remember that ginormous gator that was in the road that time?" Jax said.

When Delta was about nine years old, they had all been driving home from dinner out one night. When they pulled into Palmetto Dunes, a big old alligator stretched nearly across the whole road. It was just lying there, enjoying the heat that the road had been soaking up all day. Pops had to keep honking his horn until that old gator finally looked up at them. You could just about hear it sigh before it turned around and crawled back across the road and slid into the canal so the car could pass.

Delta smiled as everyone else laughed at the memory.

"He was a big old boy, wasn't he?" Pops said.

"Yes, but I bet we wouldn't have been laughing so hard if we hadn't had the car doors between us and him!" Tootsie said.

Once seated in the restaurant, Delta picked up the menu and read "The Port Royal Inn." The food was mostly fancy stuff, but fortunately there was a kid's menu that offered fish sandwiches, chicken strips, and burgers. Ordinarily, Delta didn't like to order from the children's menu anymore, but sometimes it really did offer better choices. She ordered a cheeseburger and fries.

While they waited for their food to arrive, Tootsie suggested they head to the lookout deck.

"What the heck is that?" Jax asked.

"This building used to be an old hotel," Pops explained. "There's a lookout tower up on top, so sailors staying at the inn could climb up there and see if ships were coming into port."

"Or their ladies could watch and see if they were returning from sea," Tootsie added.

The family climbed up a narrow winding staircase in the center of the restaurant and ended up in a small room surrounded by windows. A door led to a deck, which Pops said the current owners of the restaurant had added so people could get an even better, 360-degree view.

From the deck, Delta could see the choppy waters of Port Royal Sound spreading into the distance. Far on the other side, like an optical illusion, she could barely make out a stripe of darkness on the horizon line that indicated another island across the bay. Glancing slightly to her right, she saw the open Atlantic Ocean.

"What's that, Pops?" Jax asked.

Delta turned to see that he was looking in the opposite direction. At first she only saw a scattered forest of palmetto and live oak trees, but then she noticed strange hills here and there on the property next door to the restaurant.

"That's what's left of Fort Walker," Pops said. "It was built about 150 years ago. The Confederates used it to protect Port Royal Sound from Union ships."

At the mention of "Fort Walker," Delta and Jax immediately turned to stare at each other. That was the place mentioned on Jax's cloth!

"Can we go check it out?" Jax asked, wide-eyed.

"After dinner," Tootsie said. "Our food's probably already sitting at the table getting cold!"

The family headed carefully back down the circular staircase and saw that Tootsie was right. The food looked and smelled delicious, but Delta and Jax hardly noticed its taste in their rush to eat. In fact, Jax even turned down dessert, which wasn't like him at all.

Delta knew he just wanted to hurry up and get to the ruins next door. To be honest, she was kind of anxious to go exploring, too.

After the week they'd been having, there was no telling what they might discover at Fort Walker!

* * * *

When Delta imagined a fort, she pictured logs standing up on end side by side, maybe with points on top—like a row of sharpened pencils. Fort Walker was nothing like that. As the family approached the lot next door to the restaurant, there were no wooden walls anywhere. The ruins of the old fort consisted of a flat central area, surrounded on three sides by a sort of wall made of long, flat-topped mounds of earth.

"Did the fort's walls used to be on top of those hills?" Jax asked.

"Nope," Pops said. "Those hills *were* the walls. The soldiers had cannons up there aimed out to sea. See, here's some information on it."

Pops pointed out a fiberglass sign that told about the site.

"Fort Walker," Delta read. She skimmed through the paragraphs below, and then stopped short.

"The fort was taken by the Union Army during the Battle of Port Royal," the sign said, "on November 7, 1861."

That was the exact date on Jax's cloth message!

Delta turned to tell her brother what she had discovered, but it turned out he had seen a set of steps leading up the side of the wall and was already near the top.

"Hey, Jax!" she yelled.

She headed up the stairs after him, with Pops and Tootsie following behind.

"Stay on the path, Jackson!" Pops called. "There's plenty of poison ivy around here, and we don't want you getting into it!"

Jax looked back over his shoulder and rolled his eyes.

"Geez! I'm a Boy Scout, Pops! I know what poison ivy looks like!"

From the top of the mound, Delta could make out the fort's long, bending shape. It kind of reminded her of a giant, jungly snake with a narrow dirt path lining its back. To her left she could see the flat, sunken area where she had just read the sign. To her right, the evening sunlight sparkled on Port Royal Sound. At the base of the fort's dirt wall, a deep ditch followed the curving shape.

"That was the moat," Pops explained. "When they dug all the dirt to build this mound, it left a moat that they filled with water."

"Did it keep enemies out?" Delta asked.

Pops laughed.

"I don't know about that," he said, "but I bet it bred a lot of mosquitoes!"

Delta glanced across the top of the fort and saw Jax far ahead of her. Carefully keeping her eyes to the path, Delta avoided the encroaching poison ivy as she headed toward her brother.

"Hey, wait up, Jax!"

She looked up to see how far ahead of her he was, but she did a double-take when she saw the boy in the distance. Instead of cargo shorts and a t-shirt, this kid had patched pants and a baggy old shirt.

Was that Patchy kid stalking them or something?

Delta spun around to find Jax. Had he noticed Patchy, too?

She saw Tootsie and Pops back by the stairs, sitting on a bench next to the path, looking out at the water. Spinning in the other direction, she saw Jax climbing on an old cannon, oblivious to anyone else. Patchy stood about halfway between the two siblings, staring straight at Delta.

"Hey, Jax!" she called, waving her arms to get his attention.

She didn't notice that she had wandered off the path. She didn't feel the ivy tickling her ankles, or the spider that had just crawled onto her foot. In her excitement to point out Patchy to her brother, Delta didn't see the danger she had placed herself in until it was too late.

One moment she was waving to Jax, and the next Delta was plunging into darkness, the ground beneath her feet falling away into nothingness.

9

Feeling the Way

"Oh my goodness! Is she alright?"

Delta could hear the muffled sound of Tootsie's voice. The girl had screamed as she fell, drawing the attention of her grandparents and her brother, who were now apparently overhead somewhere.

Delta coughed and rubbed her eyes. The air around her was dusty and stale, smelling of earth and rotten wood. She blinked and tried to see where she was, but the small shaft of evening light was not bright enough to illuminate her surroundings.

"Delta, honey! Are you hurt!" Pops called. He sounded as if he were directly above her somewhere.

"I . . . I don't think so," she replied, not really sure.

She felt her arms, legs, and face for anything that felt like it was bleeding. She had landed on a fairly hard surface, but the dirt and vines she had been standing on had apparently cushioned her fall. She was a little sore, but nothing seemed broken.

"No, I think I'm okay," she called up to her grandparents. "But where am I?"

"I think you fell through the roof of an old Civil War bomb shelter," Pops said. "They built them into the walls of the fort for protection in case an enemy was shooting cannons at them."

"Cool!" Jax chimed in.

Delta's eyes had adjusted a bit to the dim light in her cramped quarters, and when she looked up she could see the outline of Pops' and Jax's heads peering over the edge of the hole about 15 feet above her. She stood up, but could not reach the top. Pops stretched his arm as far into the hole as he could, but their fingertips did not even touch.

"Don't worry, kiddo. We'll get you out of there," he said. "I'll go see if they've got a ladder we could use over at the restaurant."

"I'm coming with you!" Jax yelled.

"No, you stay and keep Tootsie and your sister company."

Pops' head disappeared and Tootsie's replaced it.

"Oh, my stars!" Tootsie called down. "How in the world did this happen?"

"Delta didn't stay on the path like you said."

"Now, Jax, don't you go trying to stir up more trouble," Tootsie replied.

Delta looked around her and tried to make out what she saw. The dust from her fall was settling a bit, and she could see rough dirt walls, with a few wooden beams framing out the space. Part of the collapsed roof leaned against the wall behind her. The wood looked really old, and when she poked it, it was soft to her touch. The space she was in seemed about the size of a small bathroom. How many soldiers were supposed to hide in here during a battle?

Delta could hear Jax and Tootsie bickering above her. Weren't they supposed to be there to make her feel better? The girl sighed, and then noticed a strange sensation on her face. Cool air was blowing from somewhere, but where?

In the dim light from above, she could see that the settling dust wasn't just moving down, toward the ground, but to the right. That meant air was coming in from the left. Delta inched in that direction, her arms outstretched. As she moved away from the hole above her, the darkness grew thicker until she could not see her own hand in front of her face. She could feel the old dirt walls of the enclosure, though, and, following them, realized that her initial assessment of the space didn't do it justice. Behind the collapsed roof from her fall, the bomb shelter extended much farther. She felt her way along as far as she could until she felt cool air blowing directly in her face.

Delta placed her hand on the tiny opening, surprised to find that she was no longer touching dirt walls. The area in front of her was a mass of vines. She imagined that this spot had once been the doorway to the shelter, but, over the past 150 years, the surrounding foliage had braided itself together until it formed a wall of its own.

She squeezed her hand through the opening and grabbed a handful of plants, tugging as hard as she could. A rope of vines gave way, making the hole a bit larger. Delta pulled at the plants with both hands now, enlarging the opening with each effort. Before long, she had created a hole large enough to step through.

Climbing out into the fading evening light, Delta squinted and brushed dust and dirt from her hair with her hands. She soaked in the twilight and fresh air that flooded over her as she gained her bearings. She could see that she was at the bottom of the wall of the fort, and could hear voices from the top.

"She just disappeared!" Delta heard Jax say. "The ground just swallowed her up!"

Delta made her way around to the steps that they'd originally climbed, and joined the group—which apparently now included onlookers from the restaurant—up near the hole. In the growing darkness, though, and in the midst of all the excitement, no one noticed her approach.

"Do you think she's okay?" a stranger asked.

"She said she was, when she first fell," Tootsie replied, "but now we haven't heard anything at all from her in quite a while!"

"I . . ." Delta began, but was interrupted by another sight-seer.

"They should make these places safer. I'd sue, if I were you."

"But, I'm . . ." Delta tried again.

"Yeah, let's sue!" Jax said. "We can use the money to save the museum!"

"There won't be any lawsuits, Jackson," Pops said. "It was just an accident."

A man with a ladder joined the group.

"Move aside, folks," he said. "Let me get this down there so we can survey the damage."

"Oh, my dear!" Tootsie said. "I bet the poor thing has fainted from fear!"

"Yep," Delta was finally able to add. "She's a goner, for sure."

"Delta?" Jax said, recognizing his sister's voice in the darkness.

She began laughing.

"I'm fine! I found a way out, but you guys wouldn't stop gabbing long enough for me to tell you!"

The group gave a collective sigh of relief, followed by nervous laughter.

Pops gently held Delta by the shoulders and examined her for any injuries.

"You sure you're all right?" he asked.

Delta stretched her arms, and then her legs. She turned her head from one side to the other.

"Yeah, I'm good."

"That was awesome! You just disappeared, like that!" Jax said with a snap of his fingers.

Delta laughed, a mixture of nervousness and relief.

"Well, at least I didn't get hit by any cannon balls!" she said.

* * * *

After taking a hot shower to rinse off all the bomb shelter dust, Delta changed into her pajamas and was getting into bed when Jax burst into her room.

"Look what I've got!" he shouted, waving something wildly in the air. "Pops helped me make it!"

"What *is* that thing?" Delta asked.

Jax extended his arm toward his sister. In his hand, he held some sort of wooden handle, studded with razor-sharp shark teeth on one side.

"It's a hatchet. Pops showed me how to carve a groove in the side, and then we stuck some shark teeth we found at the beach into the groove."

Delta could see that they had sewn the teeth in place with some type of cord.

Jax swung the hatchet menacingly at an imaginary foe, giving a karate chop sound in the process.

"How do you expect to get that through security at the airport?" Delta asked.

"I'm going to put it in my checked luggage," Jax shrugged.

Delta shook her head.

"Mom and Dad are *never* going to let you keep that."

"Uh huh," Jax replied. "Pops says Native Americans used to make this kind of weapon all the time around here. It's historical and *educational.*"

Delta rolled her eyes. Mom was always wanting the kids to do *educational* things.

"Well, just keep it away from me," she said.

But then she remembered that, what with the excitement of her fall and everything, she had forgotten to tell Jax about what she had discovered at Fort Walker.

"Hey, wait a minute," she said, before he could leave her doorway. "I meant to tell you something I saw at the fort."

Intrigued, Jax came back into the room and hopped onto the end of the daybed.

"What'd you see?"

"Well, while you were running around playing, I actually read the information sign and learned something kind of amazing."

She smiled and waited before she spoke again.

"What?" Jax finally asked.

"Apparently, Fort Walker was used by the Confederate Army during the Civil War until the Battle of Port Royal. That's when the Union Army took over the island."

"Okay," Jax said. "What's so amazing about that?"

"Guess when the Battle of Port Royal took place?" Delta asked.

"How should I know? During the 1800's?"

Delta grinned.

"More specifically, the battle took place on *November 7, 1861*," she said. "Sound familiar?"

She watched Jax's face as he processed this information and realization dawned.

"Whoa!" he replied. "That's the date from the message in the bottle!"

"Exactly!" Delta said triumphantly. "That can't be a coincidence!"

"You think the letter was written *because* of the battle?"

"It makes sense," Delta said. "The message said they were under attack, didn't it? They were definitely under attack during the Battle of Port Royal."

"I think we may be onto something!" Jax said, nodding.

"Oh, and I saw Patchy at the fort before I fell," Delta added. "I think he's following us for some reason."

"Why would he be following us?" Jax asked.

"Who knows? But that kid's starting to give me the creeps."

Bursting in Air

Delta slathered herself in sunblock and lay back on the blanket, a beach towel rolled up under her neck for a pillow. Pops had strolled across the sand to visit with a friend, and Tootsie had fallen asleep in a folding chair, a bright red floppy hat shading her face from the sun. A small American flag waved from the brim of her hat to celebrate the Fourth of July holiday.

"Okay, so down to business!" Jax whispered, plopping down beside her.

Delta rolled her eyes beneath her sunglasses.

"So we know *when* the message was written, and we know *where* it was written," Jax said. "But we still have to figure out where the treasure is!"

"If there even *is* a treasure," Delta said.

"Of course there's a treasure!" Jax countered. "'Jasper's Gems can be found under the Light of Hilton Head arch.' It says so right here in the message."

"We don't have any idea what 'Jasper's Gems' are. That could be the name of a boat or something."

"It is *not* a boat. I just know it's a treasure," Jax said. "I just do."

A shadow fell over Delta and she lifted her sunglasses to see Travis standing over her with a boogie board under his arm.

"I saw y'all's picture in the paper," the teenager said. "Did you actually touch that skeleton?"

Delta shrugged, hoping her casual look hid her pounding heartbeat.

"Yeah, it was pretty gross."

"Cool," Travis nodded.

Delta couldn't believe he would even talk to her, let alone think she was cool. The seconds ticked past as she considered what to say next. Eventually, Travis spoke.

"What's that you got there?"

This was directed at Jax, who had the old piece of cloth sitting in his lap.

"None of your beeswax!" Jax said, stuffing the cloth under his hip.

Travis just laughed.

"Whatever," he said, turning to walk away.

Delta couldn't let their encounter end like this, with him thinking she was just some goofy kid like her brother. She sat up quickly, letting her sunglasses fall to the blanket. She rolled her eyes and laughed.

"My stupid brother thinks he's found some kind of treasure map!" she said.

"Delta!" Jax slammed his fist into her thigh, but she shoved his hand away and widened her eyes at him before turning her attention back to Travis.

"He thinks he's going to find treasure on the island that'll save the history museum," she said, adding a quick laugh for effect.

Travis laughed back.

"Yeah, well," he said, "you keep me posted on that."

He turned and walked toward the surf.

"I can't believe you told him that, Delta!" Jax said. "This was supposed to be *our* secret, for Pops! Swear you won't tell anyone else. SWEAR it."

"Okay, okay! I swear it," Delta said, with a roll of her eyes.

Why were little brothers such a pain in the butt?

* * * *

After her nap, Tootsie unpacked the picnic food. Fried chicken, pimiento cheese sandwiches, watermelon cut into the shape of little stars, and cupcakes frosted with white icing and sprinkled with red and blue sparkly sugar. She handed each of them a cup of cold sweet tea and a napkin with an American flag design. Everyone was quiet as they enjoyed their patriotic feast.

Delta looked around and noticed that, little by little, other islanders were arriving at the beach. The crowd was not heavy, but was getting there.

After filling up on their picnic, the kids jumped waves in the ocean for a while. When they returned to their grandparents, they looked around and realized that the beach was nearly full of people spreading blankets and setting up chairs. The sounds of laughter and conversation filled the air. Here and there, groups of people were tossing Frisbees or passing footballs over the heads of the crowd.

Everywhere there was a sense of expectation. It reminded Delta of a surprise birthday party, right before the guest of honor arrives.

As the sun began its final descent, a boy wearing a glow-necklace attached a second one around his dog's neck. As the boy walked toward the shoreline, Delta noticed that he had a plastic water bottle with a glow-stick inside. He threw the glowing bottle into the surf and the dog leaped after it joyfully. In the near-darkness, she could see the dog—and the bottle—return to the boy, who tossed the bottle again. Delta laughed a little and pointed out the game to the rest of her family, as the glow-in-the-dark dog pranced through the waves.

Suddenly there was a loud whistling sound behind Delta, followed by a BOOM! The crowd around her erupted in a cheer, and she spun around to see the last remnants of a firework explosion set off from a yard backing up to the beach.

Soon fireworks were lighting the sky all up and down the shore. As soon as one rocket would burst, another would shoot off a few doors down.

"There're too many to see!" Jax said, jumping up and down excitedly.

"Then follow me!" Pops said, motioning for the family to join him.

All four of them waded into the surf until they were up to their waists in the water. They turned their backs to the horizon and looked back toward the island. Fireworks filled the sky! Red, blue, white, green, yellow! With the displays reflected on the water's surface, it was as if they swam in a sea of colorful flower blossoms. The bursts were over them, around them, and engulfed them.

Delta looked around her at Tootsie laughing and clapping her hands. Pops looking happier than he had in days, pointing excitedly from one to another bursting rocket. Jax was still jumping up and down, splashing them all with salt water with each leap.

Delta's smile dimmed as she flashed back to another night on these same waters. Bombs burst overhead then, too, but with deadlier results. On that fateful November night over 150 years ago, ships in Port Royal Sound had been the ones shooting off rockets, and those on shore were not "ooh-ing" and "aah-ing" over them. Those fireworks meant war.

The message Jax had found was written because of that battle. But who was Colonel William Wagener? What were Jasper's Gems? And why had Colonel Wagener believed it was so important for someone to find them?

Facing the Facts

"Rise and shine, Delta-Boo! You're going on an adventure!"

Delta opened her eyes a slit and saw Tootsie standing over her with a big grin on her face.

"What kind of adventure?" Delta mumbled, rubbing the sleep out of her eyes.

"Well, y'all've been awfully patient with me spending all my time working on the art fair, so we figured you'd earned a treat. Pops is meeting with the Historical Commission in Columbia tonight, and he thought you and your brother might like to go along. If you kiddos get up pronto, you'll have time to take a detour to Charleston first and stop by the State Archaeological Museum.

That caught Delta's attention.

"You mean, the one that's examining the skeleton?"

"That's right," Tootsie responded with a twinkle in her eye. "Pops thought you might be interested in what they've figured out about your discovery."

That *would* be pretty cool.

"Pack a change of clothes and some pajamas in your backpack," Tootsie said, "You'll spend the night in Columbia."

Tootsie spun around when she reached the door of the room.

"Oh! I almost forgot!" she said. "I have another surprise for you!"

Tootsie held out her hand and Delta stared blankly at what it held.

"I know you were disappointed about your phone, so I thought you could just use mine for the summer," Tootsie said. "I never use the thing, so you might as well get some good out of it."

Delta reached out and took the old flip phone.

"Does it text?" she asked.

"Oh, heavens, I don't know about that," Tootsie said. "But you can make calls with it in case of emergencies and what-not. That's the important thing."

"Gee, thanks, Tootsie," Delta said, smiling weakly.

Delta watched her grandmother leave the room and head down the hall.

"Wake up, Jax! You're headed for adventure!" Tootsie said.

* * * *

The kids packed in no time and scarfed down their breakfast, eager to get on their way. Before they could leave the island, though, Pops had to stop by the museum to pick up some important papers or something he needed to show the Historical Commission.

"You kiddos should check out the museum," Pops said. "I'll be a few minutes."

Delta wandered through the old plantation house's familiar rooms. The Nature Room had displays about the beach and the forest and the salt marsh. Stuffed wading birds stood here and there as if they had just wandered in from Broad Creek. One area of the room focused on hurricanes and had photos showing storm damage on the island like a hundred years ago. Funny how trees and vines had grown back until you couldn't tell there'd ever been a hurricane at all.

Another room was all about the history of the museum property itself. Displays there talked about plantation life and farming. There were some samples of Sea Island cotton that you could touch. They looked like bigger versions of the cotton balls you get at the drug store, except with dried brown leaves and stems.

One exhibit talked all about slavery, and showed photos and quotes by those who used to work the land right by the museum. It was hard for Delta to imagine that people lived here as prisoners, basically, and were forced to work. Even little kids. It made her ashamed, somehow, even though she hadn't even been alive then.

As she was leaving the room, Delta noticed a small display half-hidden behind an open door. "The Civil War on Hilton Head Island," the heading read. She pulled the door back enough to see the entire exhibit, which really only consisted of a large framed poster with writing and a bunch of really old photos in varying shades of brown.

Delta skimmed through the text until she got to a paragraph about the Battle of Port Royal. It talked about Confederate forces being there first, and then the Union forces moving in and taking over. All stuff Delta already knew.

But then she saw a name she recognized.

"'Among those killed during the battle was the leader of Fort Walker, Colonel William Wagener,'" Delta read out loud.

The guy who wrote Jax's message!

Delta furrowed her eyebrows in thought, and then opened her eyes wide as she realized the implications of what she had just read.

"He must've written that message right before he died!" she said in a whisper.

But, if he died in the battle at Fort Walker, how did his message end up over in the marsh? They were a couple of miles apart.

"Hey, Jax!" she called. "Come look what I found."

Delta turned and saw Jax stuffing the wads of Sea Island cotton in his ears.

"Gross, Jax! Put those down!" she said loudly, hoping he could hear her through the cotton.

Laughing, he put the cotton back on the table and spun around toward Delta.

"Watch out!" she shouted.

The display case next to him held a model ship, complete with tiny rigging and sails. It must have taken someone forever to build it.

As if in slow motion, Delta saw her brother bang right into the display, knocking the boat off its stand. She held her breath as the glass case itself teetered precariously.

"Get away from my ship!" an angry voice yelled at them.

Delta looked up to see Captain DeFoe standing menacingly in the doorway to the room, his face red with rage. Before the kids knew what was happening, he was racing toward them, waving his metallic hook of a hand.

12

Sharing the Secret

Jax and Delta couldn't move, they were so stunned. They watched helplessly as the display case rattled and rocked, finally settling back into position. Although the boat had fallen off its perch, at least the glass hadn't broken.

"Look what you've done!" the Captain screeched. "You've broken the rigging!"

"Sorry," Jax said meekly.

"Sorry's not gonna fix my ship! You kids get on outta here before I give you something to be sorry about!"

Without hesitation, Delta and Jax hurried out onto the front porch and sat down on the steps.

"It was just an accident," Jax said.

"How dare he talk to us like that!" Delta added. "He knows our grandfather runs this place!"

"Yeah!"

Jax was starting to feel braver now that they were no longer in the same room with the angry old man.

"Just 'cause he's a Captain doesn't mean he's in charge of us!" he said. "What's his problem, anyway?"

"Y'all don't know about the Captain?"

Delta looked up with a start, surprised to see Travis standing in front of them with a pair of hedge trimmers in his hand.

"We know he's mean!" Jax said.

"Not just mean," Travis said with a sigh and a shake of his head. "That guy's crazy. Certifiably insane."

"No way," Delta said. "Pops wouldn't hire him if he were really insane."

"Your grandpa thought the Captain was cured when he hired him, but now everyone's just scared of what he might do if he gets fired."

"Really?" Jax asked, his head tilted to one side. "I don't know. . . ."

Travis propped one foot on the bottom step and rested his arms on his raised knee. He looked around to make sure no one was in earshot.

"Listen, your grandparents didn't want y'all to know this because they didn't want to scare you," he said. "But I think you have a right to know. I mean, you're in danger every time you're around that guy."

"What kind of danger?" Delta asked.

"The *bad* kind," Travis said, widening his eyes.

"What do you mean?" Jax asked.

"Well, I might as well tell you the whole story. Everyone else on the island knows it."

Delta and Jax leaned forward to catch Travis's every word.

"You see, he didn't start out crazy," he began. "When he was young, he was just your average fisherman, with a nice little boat and a few guys in his crew. But then the storm hit."

"The storm?" Jax asked, wide-eyed.

"Yep, the storm of the century. Everyone believed the Captain's boat had gone down in the storm, and it had. His crew disappeared, and there was even a funeral for the Captain. But then, three weeks later, a shrimper found him floating in a lifeboat out at sea, dehydrated and hallucinating."

"Hallucinating?" Delta asked.

"That's right. He was convinced he was a pirate, and that his crew had mutinied—you know, kicked him off the ship."

"That's crazy," Jax said.

"Exactly. Everybody thought he'd get back to normal once he recovered from being in the lifeboat so long, though. He seemed like he was getting better for a while. But then there was that one night."

Travis shook his head sadly.

"What happened?" Delta asked.

"Well, I don't want to freak y'all out, but you deserve to know. One night in a fit of craziness he cut off his own hand, just so he could get a hook hand, like a real pirate."

"No one would do that!" Delta said, rolling her eyes.

"No *sane* person would do it!" Travis replied. "Not long after that, fisherman all over the island started disappearing."

He looked from Delta to Jax, then nodded.

"Turns out the Captain believed they were pirates, too. *Rival* pirates. He had killed every last one of them."

"Whoa!" Jax said.

"That's when they sent him to the insane asylum. He was there for years and years. He finally convinced his doctors that he wasn't crazy anymore, so they let him out. That's when your grandpa hired him here at the museum."

"A crazy guy?" Delta said.

"Well, you've got to remember, he claimed he was all cured, and his doctors believed him. Your grandpa wanted to give the guy a chance at a new life."

"That does sound like something Pops would do," Jax said to Delta, and she had to agree.

"So he's not crazy anymore," Delta said.

"He doesn't want people to *think* he's crazy anymore," Travis corrected. "But trust me. I'm around him all the time, and I swear he still thinks he's a pirate. Why do you suppose he insists everyone call him 'Captain.' He believes he's a pirate, alright. And not a nice pirate, either."

Delta thought back to the picture in Pops' office of the Captain with a parrot on his arm. And he did have that hook hand. It wasn't like a Captain Hook type hook, more a modern-looking mechanical one, but still. They probably didn't make the Peter Pan kind anymore.

"He did think that boat I knocked over was his ship," Jax said.

"See! What'd I tell you?" Travis said. "He thinks it's his pirate ship."

"The guys' crazy, I tell you. And a murderer," he added. "There's no telling what could set him off, or what he might do next."

"I don't know . . . " Delta said.

Just then, a door at the far end of the porch opened and the Captain himself stepped out. The kids immediately stopped talking and watched silently as he pulled a flat brown bottle from the back pocket of his filthy pants. Twisting the top off, he tilted the bottle to his mouth and took a big swig of its contents, then capped it and stuck it back in his pocket. He stepped off the end of the porch and headed away from the building.

Travis raised his eyebrows knowingly.

"See? What'd I tell you?" he asked. "Yo ho ho, and a bottle of rum."

Delta watched the Captain disappear into the distance.

No wonder Pops had told them to stay out of his way. That guy was crazy.

13

Soaking the Bones

Delta and Jax were relieved when Pops appeared on the porch of the museum and announced it was time to hit the road. They couldn't stop thinking about what Travis had told them.

"Why are y'all so quiet?" Pops asked.

"No reason," Jax said quickly, glancing sideways at Delta. "We're just excited about our trip, I guess."

It was only a couple of hours' drive up the Atlantic coast to Charleston. Pops took back roads that took them through tunnels of live oak trees dripping with Spanish moss. Every now and then, they'd cross a bridge over a marshy area that was carved with the winding path of a tidal creek.

As they entered the busier city streets, Delta could see that Charleston was definitely *not* a city like Chicago. First of all, it was much smaller. Pops explained that the whole downtown part of the city was situated on a peninsula on Charleston Harbor.

"When I was younger, I could walk across the whole city," Pops said. "It's only a few square miles—smaller than Hilton Head, actually."

Delta also noticed that Charleston looked really old. There were hardly any tall buildings, not like the skyscrapers in her hometown, anyway. Instead, these narrow streets were lined with shops, restaurants, and office buildings only a few stories high. There were lots of houses, too, which you didn't see in downtown Chicago. These houses were huge, though, with lots of big shady porches on every level. Hanging baskets of flowers and ferns swung in the summer breeze around the edges of the porch ceilings.

"Are those apartment buildings?" Delta asked.

"Some of them have been turned into apartments," Pops said. "And some are bed and breakfast inns, like hotels. But some of them are still home to just one family."

The houses were all painted in pretty pastel colors—pale pink, green, lavender, blue, yellow. Some were painted white, with colorful trim. They made Delta think of fancy birthday cakes.

Pops pulled his truck into a parking space next to a tall stone wall.

"Is this it?" Jax asked, looking around. "Where's the museum?"

There was a tree-filled park next to them, with a big gazebo in the middle. Delta saw some old mounted cannons at one end of the park, but no museum building.

"They're not expecting us at the museum for a while," Pops told them. "I thought we'd have a picnic first."

He flipped the back of the truck down and pulled out a cooler and blanket. The kids found a flat spot under a shady magnolia tree where they could enjoy the sandwiches Tootsie had packed for them.

"Hey, what are those people doing on top of that wall?" Jax asked, pointing toward their parking place. "How'd they get up there?"

Delta saw that lots of people were on top of the wall, some strolling along and others standing, looking at something in the distance.

"Let's pack up our trash and go see!" Pops said with a wink.

After disposing of the wrappings from their lunch in a nearby garbage can, the trio returned the blanket and cooler to the truck bed. The siblings followed their grandfather down the street a ways until they came to a set of narrow stone steps set into the side of the wall. Delta clutched nervously at the side of the stairwell as they began their ascent, bemoaning the fact that there was no handrail. Heights were *not* her favorite. After climbing ten feet or so, though, Delta reached the top and gasped.

Charleston Harbor spread out before them in all its glory. Sunlight shimmered on the water and reflected off boats and ships of all types and sizes. Sailboats and speedboats plied the waters, while a cruise ship headed toward land. Passing it, an enormous cargo liner chugged in the direction of the open ocean, carrying train cars stacked like building blocks.

"Ooh! Can we ride that?" Jax asked.

Families on the top deck of a medium-sized boat waved as they sailed past them. "Charleston Harbor Tours" was painted in bright red on the side of the boat.

"Not this time, buddy," Pops said. "I'm afraid we don't have time for that."

"But why not?" Jax said. "It's looks so fun!"

"Yes, but that boat goes out to Fort Sumter for the afternoon. We have an appointment to check out the skeleton."

"Fort Sumter?" Jax asked.

Pops pointed toward the ocean-end of the harbor.

"See that island out there—with the American flag flying?"

Delta squinted into the midday sun and saw the spit of land and the flag.

"Where's the fort?" she asked.

"Well, there's not much fort left," Pops said. "It was originally built to defend our country from England in the Battle of 1812. Then the Union Army took control of it just before the Civil War, and the folks around here didn't like that much. The first shots of the Civil War were aimed at that fort, and then the Confederate Army ended up shooting cannons over there and nearly demolished it. It's a National Park now."

"They ruined their own fort?" Jax asked.

"Yep. It was father against son and brother against brother in that war, you know," Pops said with a sigh. "A lot of families were split right down the middle with their loyalties to either the North or the South."

Delta watched the flag waving proudly in the breeze on the little island across the harbor and tried to imagine cannon balls soaring across this scenic view. She and Jax were from the North, and her grandparents were from the South. How awful it would be if that distinction meant they had to be enemies!

As if he could read her mind, Pops caught Delta's eye.

"'Time Machine', huh?" he said with a wink.

"I'm glad we live now and not back then," Delta said as the family headed carefully back down the steps to street level.

"Me, too," Pops said, and gave his granddaughter a big hug before they all piled back into the truck.

* * * *

When the family arrived at the State Archaeological Museum, they were immediately ushered back to a laboratory where a couple of scientists in white lab coats were huddled over what looked like a large fish tank. A young woman wearing goggles looked up at them and smiled.

"You must be the great discoverers!" she said, pulling off a rubber glove and extending her hand toward Delta for a handshake. "I'm Dr. Chang."

After introductions, Dr. Chang allowed the family to approach the tank, which Delta could now see was only a few inches deep—just enough that the skeleton inside was completely immersed in water. The girl hesitated at first, not sure how she would feel seeing the skull again, but she found herself fascinated by the work the scientists had done. Not only were the bones all cleaned, but they had been arranged in the bottom of the tank in the shape of a body.

Delta felt a chill run down her spine. Where the body's head belonged, she spied the skull that, not so long ago, she had held in her hand.

"Since the skeleton was preserved in the mud and salt water for so many years, we're keeping it submerged in a saline solution most of the time while we do our initial research," Dr. Chang explained. "Eventually, we'll let the bones dry for storage or display."

Delta swallowed hard, feeling a bit nauseous. That poor person had been trapped in the marsh for over a hundred years, and now was *still* soaking in water!

"Who was it?" Jax asked.

"They can't tell that from just bones, Jax," Delta said with a roll of her eyes.

Dr. Chang just smiled.

"Actually, we can tell a lot more than you think," she said. "We've determined that this skeleton belonged to a boy between the ages of 12 and 14. He lived about 150 years ago, and was about 5 feet 3 inches tall."

"Whoa!" Jax said.

"You can tell all that?" Delta added.

"Yes, ma'am," Dr. Chang replied.

Replacing her rubber glove, she picked up a long tool of some sort and pointed at a hole in the skeleton's upper right leg.

"See that right there?" she asked.

As everyone nodded, she turned to a table behind them. When she spun back around, she held a clear plastic box in her hand.

"What *is* that?" Jax said, asking the question on everyone's mind.

"It's the bullet that was in that boy's leg," Dr. Chang said. "A Civil War-era bullet."

"So he died of a gunshot wound?" Delta asked.

"No, not likely," the scientist answered. "A bullet wound in the leg would have been very painful, and eventually he may have bled a lot, but it probably would not have killed him."

"So how did he die?" Jax asked.

"Unfortunately, we can't be sure of that. Since he was in the water, he may have drowned, although I understand that you found him in only a couple of feet of water."

"That's right," Delta nodded.

She gazed at the remains of the boy in the tank. He had been about her age when his life ended. Surely he had been too young to be a soldier. And yet he had died with a soldier's bullet in his leg. Delta thought of the boys her age that she knew from school. She couldn't imagine any of them fighting in a war. Or dying.

Who was this boy?

If only Delta could know his story. Now, *that* would be quite the game of "Time Machine"!

* * * *

Dr. Chang handed Pops a bright yellow file folder.

"Here are the results of all the testing we've done so far," she said. "You might find some of this data interesting."

"Absolutely!" he replied. "I'm fascinated by the whole dating process."

Delta stifled a laugh. She knew Pops was curious about determining the age of the skeleton, but to a kid her age, his statement meant something totally different!

Dr. Chang waited patiently while Pops read through the pages of material.

Suddenly, though, the silence was broken by a loud rumble from Jax's belly.

"Nice, Jax," Delta said, rolling her eyes. "Excuse you!"

"I can't help it," he said, rubbing his stomach. "I'm hungry."

"Jackson, we just ate lunch before we got here!" Pops said.

"Well, I'm a growing boy," Jax replied with a shrug. "I need constant fuel."

Pops sighed, but Dr. Chang smiled and offered a solution.

"We have vending machines at the end of the hallway, if you'd like to get a snack."

Pops dug some change out of his pocket and handed it to his grandson.

"Delta, you go with your brother so he doesn't get into too much trouble," Pops said.

Delta groaned, but followed Jax out of the lab and down the hall to a row of machines offering canned drinks and junk food. After debating between getting salty or sweet, the boy finally decided on a bag of cheddar cheese-flavored popcorn.

With Jax munching on his new treat, the duo headed back toward the lab where their grandfather and Dr. Chang were likely still in deep discussion about the aging of skeletons. Before they reached that room, though, Delta saw a sign on a different doorway.

"Jax! Look at this!"

The sign on the door said, "H. L. Hunley Restoration Lab—Authorized Personnel Only."

"What's the Hummly?" Jax asked.

"The *H. L. Hunley,*" Delta corrected. "Can't you read? It was the first submarine in history to sink an enemy ship. I saw a movie about it at school."

"So what's it doing here?" the boy asked.

"It sank just outside Charleston Harbor during the Civil War, so I guess they brought it here to restore it."

"No way," Jax replied, shaking his head. "They didn't have submarines way back then."

"Yes, they did. Just not as big or safe as the ones we have today. My history teacher said the *Hunley* sank three different times."

"How is that even possible?" Jax asked. "Once a ship has sunk it's pretty much done, isn't it?"

"Well, you'd think so," Delta said. "But the first two times the *Hunley* sank, they knew right where it was and were able to pull it back up. They lost it the third time, though, because they didn't know where to find it."

"But somebody eventually figured it out?" Jax asked.

Delta nodded.

"In the movie this treasure-hunter guy found the sub on the bottom of the ocean like 20 years ago or something, but it's taken this long to raise it and get all the gunk off."

"Cool!" Jax said, pushing the door open and walking right in.

"Jax!" Delta whispered viciously as she followed her brother into the restricted lab. "We're not allowed in here! It says 'Authorized Personnel Only'! We are not *authorized!*"

14

Grabbing a Snack

"Whoa!" Jax said, looking at the enormous glass-sided tank that rose in front of them.

The tank was over 10 feet tall and had a metal walkway built all around the top of it. Delta figured that provided access for the scientists to examine the object inside the tank. The *Hunley* itself was about as long as a school bus, but only a few feet in diameter. It looked like a big rusty hot dog.

"I thought it would be bigger," Jax said. "I guess modern submarines are way bigger than that because people have to fit inside them."

"People fit inside this one, too," Delta said. "Five people sat scrunched in that thing."

She noticed a poster board on the wall of the lab and wandered over to check it out. The handmade poster was divided into three sections, each marked in a different color and devoted to a different sailing of the *Hunley*, with names and descriptions of the crew members.

Delta scanned the lists, particularly amazed by the third crew. She couldn't believe that men would have been willing to ride on that tiny submarine after it had already sunk—not once, but twice! They had to know their chances weren't good.

A name on the third list caught Delta's eye.

"Sergeant Julius Jasper."

Huh. Like "Jasper's Gems."

She read further.

"Even prior to his service on the *H. L. Hunley*, Sergeant Jasper was already considered a Civil War hero as a result of his rescuing and replanting the fallen Confederate flag after it was shot down from Fort Walker during the Battle of Port Royal."

Whatever "Jasper's Gems" were, Jasper himself had died in a tiny Civil War submarine just outside Charleston Harbor!

"Hey, Jax, look at this!" Delta called, tapping the board where Sergeant Jasper's description was listed. "That's the guy from your message! After the battle on Hilton Head, Julius Jasper ended up sailing—and dying—on the *Hunley*."

"That's awesome!" Jax said from across the room.

"It's not awesome, Jax," Delta said. "The poor guy drowned in that metal tube."

"I know that, but don't you see what it means for us?"

Delta had no idea what her stupid brother was talking about.

"If he died, then maybe he never went back to find his gems," Jax explained. "Our chances of the treasure being there once we figure out all the clues is better than ever!"

Delta considered what her brother had said. Maybe he had a point.

"Awe, man! I missed it!" Jax added.

"What?" Delta asked, turning to see her brother toss a piece of cheesy-coated popcorn in the air.

Jax had his orange-stained chin tipped toward the ceiling, and Delta watched the popcorn hit his nose and bounce off, landing on the tiled floor near several other pieces that he had apparently already missed.

"Good one," she said, laughing. "You've got chee-dust all over your face."

"No, watch," Jax told her. "I'm really good at this. We did it all the time at Boy Scout camp."

He threw another piece of popcorn upward and actually caught this one.

"See!" he said triumphantly.

"You're going to choke."

"Watch—two in a row!" Jax said, hurling yet another of his snacks toward the ceiling.

Delta stood with her arms crossed as she saw the popcorn rise higher and higher before falling vaguely in the direction of her brother. The orange speck hit the handrail surrounding the metal walkway around the tank, bounced twice on the walkway itself, and rolled right into the water with the priceless submarine.

"Great job, Jax! Look what you've done!" Delta said.

Jax dropped the bag of popcorn on a nearby desk and climbed the metal stairs to the walkway.

"No big deal," he said. "I can get it."

The piece of misdirected popcorn was floating on top of the water in the tank. It wasn't hard to spot, even from the ground, thanks to the orange-stained ring growing around it.

"You know they probably keep that water at a particular chemical balance and stuff to preserve the sub, Jax. You're going to ruin it!"

"Take a chill pill," Jax said.

He knelt down on the edge of the walkway and stuck his arm in the tank, paddling the water toward him as if to entice the popcorn to swim back to the side. All his paddling, though, just forced the piece further into the middle of the tank.

"You're hopeless!" his sister said, climbing the stairs to join him. "You're probably going to fall in the tank with it, and I'll have to fish you both out."

She settled herself on the opposite side of the tank, leaning over and pulling the water toward her. As if mocking them, though, the piece of popcorn and its accompanying cheesy film remained safely out of reach in the middle of the enormous tank.

"This isn't working," Delta said with a sigh. "Our arms aren't long enough."

Jax sped down the steps to a nearby desk.

"What are you doing now?" his sister asked.

"Making a fishing pole!"

Delta descended the stairs and joined her brother, where he was sorting through various office supplies in the desk drawers.

"You shouldn't be going through somebody's desk," Delta said. "That's so rude!"

"I need this stuff," Jax responded.

Delta watched as he used clear packing tape to connect a ruler, several fat markers, a pair of scissors, and a coffee-stained plastic spoon end-to-end.

"Ta-da!" he said, raising his new invention triumphantly. "It's the 'Snack-Grabber 3000'!"

Delta laughed. She had to give her stupid little brother credit. Sometimes he was pretty smart.

The duo climbed back up to the walkway, where Jax held his new tool out over the surface of the water, dipping the spoon within a few inches of the floating popcorn.

"I still can't reach," he said. "You try. Your arms are longer than mine."

Delta took the Snack Grabber 3000 and aimed the tip of it at her target. Although she could reach the popcorn, though, she only succeeded in repeatedly smacking the water with the plastic spoon.

"I'm just making it float farther away!" she said.

Jax grabbed their make-shift fishing pole from his sister's hand and took it around the walkway to the other side of the tank.

"Maybe I can get it from over here," he said.

Just then, Delta heard voices outside the closed door to the lab.

"Have you had a chance to see the *Hunley* yet?" she heard Dr. Chang ask.

"Well, I've seen it before, but I was hoping to show it to my grandkids," Pops responded. "If they ever get back from the vending machines."

"Jax!" Delta whispered. "Pops is right outside the door! Get down from there! Now!"

The boy headed toward the metal stairs leading down from the elevated walkway.

"Leave the grabber, you idiot!" his sister said.

Without hesitating, Jax tossed the Snack Grabber 3000 behind him, where it landed with a splash.

Delta groaned.

Jax's new invention was floating about half-way up the tank, the weight of the scissors cancelling out the buoyancy of the plastic markers. Delta frantically looked around the room for some way to hide it, and her eyes landed on the poster she had been looking at earlier. Pulling it from the wall, she stuck it to the side of the glass tank directly in front of the floating tool, just hoping that the sticky-tac would hold it. And that the Snack Grabber 3000 didn't move. And that she and Jax could get away before anyone caught them.

But then the door to the lab swung open.

Going to College

"Delta! Jackson! What are you doing in here?" Pops said when he saw his grandkids standing in the restricted laboratory.

"We were waiting for you!" Jax said cheerfully.

"What?"

"Yeah, remember?" Delta joined in. "You said earlier that you wanted to show us the *Hunley*."

"I did?" Pops replied.

"Uh huh," Jax said. "So we figured we'd just meet you in here."

"Oh."

"Well, let me show you the sub," Dr. Chang chimed in, breaking the awkwardness of Pops' obvious confusion.

"Um, actually, we've already been looking at it while we waited," Delta said.

"Yeah," her brother added. "Very cool."

"Well, can I answer any questions about it for you?" Dr. Chang asked.

"Nope, we're good," Jax answered, heading for the door.

"Jackson!" Pops whispered with a stern look.

"Thank you," Delta told the scientist. "But we need to drive all the way to Columbia for a really important meeting tonight and you never know if traffic will be bad or something."

"You wouldn't want to be late, would you, Pops?" she added.

"I suppose not," he responded. "Maybe we should be hitting the road."

Pops and Dr. Chang led the way out the door, with Jax following behind. Delta trailed her brother, kicking a stray piece of cheddar cheese popcorn under a desk on her way. As she turned to close the door of the lab behind her, the last thing she saw was a stack of colorful markers and a plastic spoon floating through the tank past the *H. L. Hunley.*

* * * *

As Pops and the kids headed through the parking lot of the Archaeological Museum toward the truck, Delta remembered something that she had forgotten to tell her brother in all of the day's excitement.

"Hey, I saw at Pops' museum this morning that Colonel Wagener, who wrote your message, was killed during the Battle of Port Royal," she quietly told Jax as Pops walked ahead of them. "So he wouldn't have been around to find the treasure later, either."

"I just knew it!" Jax whispered. "That treasure is sitting somewhere on Hilton Head Island just waiting for us to find it!"

"Maybe," Delta said.

"No 'maybe' about it," Jax said with confidence. "We're going to find the treasure and save Pops' museum!"

* * * *

"Aaah! Feels like home!" Pops said with a contented sigh a couple of hours later.

The family was driving through the campus of the University of South Carolina in Columbia, where Pops had worked as a history professor for more than thirty years.

Pops parked the truck and led the kids through a gate in an old brick wall.

"Welcome to the Horseshoe!" Pops said, extending his arms.

A large grassy park spread in front of them, surrounded on three sides by stately-looking buildings of yellow brick. Delta figured the U-shaped arrangement explained the name "Horseshoe." Brick pathways crisscrossed the area, which was shaded by ancient live oak trees and smaller palmettos and blooming crepe myrtles of pink, red, and purple. Here and there, college-aged kids were lounging on blankets or beach towels. A couple of guys were tossing a Frisbee back and forth between them.

If this is college, Delta thought, *count me in!*

"This way," Pops said, leading the family toward one of the brick buildings.

Delta noticed a plaque on the wall as they entered that said, "Established 1804."

As soon as they entered the lobby, the family was greeted by an elderly man who enthusiastically shook Pops' hand.

"Kiddos, this is my old pal, Dr. Rutledge," their grandfather explained. "We taught here together for many fine years."

"That's right," the other man agreed. "But, unlike your grandpa here, I haven't gotten around to retiring just yet."

Pops explained to the kids that, in addition to being the head of the History Department at the university, Dr. Rutledge was a member of the State Historical Commission. He was sponsoring Pops' request for money from that organization. That meant the professor would go to tonight's meeting of the commission and basically tell his fellow members that the Island History Museum was worth saving.

"Do we all have to go to the meeting?" Delta whispered to her grandfather.

"No," Pops replied. "I believe Dr. Rutledge has made other arrangements for you and your brother."

"That's right!" Pops' friend said. "And here she comes now!"

Just then, a tall young woman with a long dark braid down her back strolled into the room, smiling broadly.

"Hi, I'm Dreema," she introduced herself, extending her hand to Pops for a shake.

She gave a small wave to Delta and Jax.

"Dreema is my research assistant," Dr. Rutledge explained. "She thought you kids might rather do something other than attend a stuffy old meeting tonight."

Anything else!

"Do you like pizza?" she asked Delta and her brother.

"Who doesn't?" Jax replied.

"Why don't you kids head off with Dreema, and I'll get settled into our rooms for the night," Pops suggested. "We'll meet back here around ten o'clock, after our meeting. How does that sound?"

Everyone agreed it was a solid plan. Pops and Dr. Rutledge headed in the direction of the car to get the luggage. Meanwhile, Dreema led Delta and Jax down a narrow pathway between two yellow brick buildings.

When they emerged on the other side, they were facing a row of modern-looking structures and a huge pool of water with numerous fountains shooting high into the air.

"Can we swim in that?" Jax asked hopefully.

Dreema laughed.

"I wish!" she said. "It's supposed to be for decoration. There are pipes and stuff on the bottom that would make it unsafe for swimming."

"Why don't we head inside for some air conditioning, though," she added.

Dreema led them into a multi-level glass-walled building and explained that it was the Student Union for the university.

"That just means it has lots of places for students to hang out," she said.

She pointed out several restaurants, a couple of stores, and even a movie theatre inside.

"How come this is all modern and the buildings on the Horseshoe look all old?" Jax asked.

"Well, when the university was first built over 200 years ago," Dreema said, "the Horseshoe was the entire school."

"Those buildings are that old?" Jax asked.

"Yes, they are," Dreema nodded. "Many more modern ones have been built since then, of course, as the university grew. Some were built to resemble the older construction, but some were designed in a more modern style—like this one."

Delta glanced around the cool interior of the Student Union, appreciating its more up-to-date features. But then, the old brick buildings and walkways held a special charm, too. She supposed there was value in both old and new.

"Why don't we check out a modern pizza restaurant?" their new friend asked with a twinkle in her eye.

Delta inhaled the delicious aromas of cheese and tomato sauce.

"Lead the way!" Jax said.

* * * *

Over pizza, Dreema explained to her guests that she was a graduate student, studying the history of the university itself. She asked each of the siblings about themselves and their interests, and listened attentively to their responses. She was especially excited at their descriptions of their hometown of Chicago, telling them that she hoped to visit that city someday.

Delta liked how, even though the young woman was an adult—probably ten years older than Delta herself—Dreema didn't treat the siblings like they were kids she had to babysit. At one point during dinner, she had received a text from a friend, but put her phone in her pocket without responding once she realized the message wasn't urgent.

"I'm hanging out with you tonight," she said with a smile and a shrug. "So what would you like to do next?"

After discussing their options, all three agreed that ice cream would sure hit the spot. Since there was an ice cream parlor right in the Student Union, it was only a few moments until the three new friends were strolling out onto the campus with huge waffle cones piled high with homemade ice cream.

Engulfed by the warm night air, Delta licked her dripping treat around the edges. She could taste the sweetness of the fresh peaches with each lick. *Yum!*

Jax had chocolate running down his right arm, and both girls laughed as they saw his giant lick, from elbow to wrist.

"No problem!" he said, with a sticky smile.

They had wandered back onto the Horseshoe, and were walking slowly along one of the brick pathways when they heard someone call out.

"Hey, Dreema!"

The trio turned in unison, but at first Delta could not see the source of the sound.

"Up here!" the voice called again.

Delta looked up to see a young man swinging in a hammock about ten feet off the ground, strung from the branches of a towering live oak tree.

"Oh, hi, Jamal!"

"Whoa!" Jax cried. "How'd you get up there!"

"Students hang hammocks in these trees all the time," Dreema explained. "These big strong branches provide great support and, as long as you don't harm the tree, the university is fine with it. It's a great place to study."

"Or take a nap!" Jamal said with a laugh.

He reached up and grabbed onto a nearby branch, swung his legs out of the hammock, and then gingerly dropped down to the ground.

"Who are your friends?" he said.

Dreema introduced everyone and explained that they were meeting Pops in an hour or so.

"Hey, I'm headed home," Jamal said, "but y'all are welcome to use my hammock for a while, if you want."

"Cool!" Jax replied.

"That'd be awesome, Jamal!" Dreema said. "I'll take it down when we're done and return it to you tomorrow."

"No rush," he replied. "Have fun!"

As Delta watched him stroll down the brick path, she noticed gas lanterns on posts lining the walkway. The sun was setting, and the shade of the gigantic trees cast an early darkness over the area. As the wind gently blew, dim light through the shifting tree branches caused flickering shapes to appear on the ground below. With most everyone gone for the day, the Horseshoe had a completely different mood at night than the cheery picnic spot it had seemed this afternoon.

Jax had finished his ice cream cone and climbed into Jamal's hammock. Delta couldn't imagine how either of them had climbed up that high to get into it. She found a fat, low-hanging branch of the tree that extended horizontally and decided that would make a fine seat for her.

"Mind if I join you?" Dreema asked.

"Sure," Delta said, scooting over a bit to make room for her new friend.

"Are you staying in a hotel tonight?" Dreema said.

"No," Delta answered. "We're actually staying in one of the apartments here on the Horseshoe. Dr. Rutledge arranged it."

Pops had explained to the kids on the ride to Columbia that while some of the buildings on the Horseshoe held classrooms and offices, others had furnished apartments in them for students. Since it was summer, many of those apartments were available.

"Hmm. Here on the Horseshoe," Dreema said slowly. "Do you know which building?"

"It's supposed to be the one next to Dr. Rutledge's office," Delta told her.

"Oooh," Dreema said, shaking her head.

"Why? What's the big deal with that?" Jax asked from high above them.

"Oh, no big deal," Dreema said, although she didn't sound like it was no big deal.

The gas lights flickered and a shadow passed in front of Delta's feet.

Dreema took a deep breath.

"You don't believe in ghosts, do you?"

16

Believing in Ghosts

"I believe in ghosts!" Jax called down from his perch in the tree branches.

Delta just laughed, but then hesitated when she saw the serious look on Dreema's face.

"Well, I hope you sleep well tonight," the graduate student said.

"Why wouldn't we?" Delta asked.

"Well, a lot has happened in these old buildings over the years, and some of the people who have stayed here . . . ."

Delta caught herself holding her breath as Dreema hesitated.

"Let's just say they haven't all left yet."

"What's that supposed to mean?" Delta asked.

Dreema sighed, and then began her story.

"I suppose I should start at the beginning. You already know that the original university consisted of these very buildings right here on the Horseshoe. That was over 200 years ago. It was just a college for men then. Most women didn't go to college."

"That's crazy!" Delta said.

"I know, right?" Dreema agreed. "Anyway, these young men went to classes, studied, lived, ate, and even went to church services right here on the Horseshoe. Everything was peaceful and fine."

"So what was the problem?" Jax asked, peering over the side of the hammock.

"No problem . . . yet," Dreema replied. "Until the Civil War came along in the 1860s. All the students headed off to fight in the war, and all these buildings were left empty, except for a few professors who stayed behind."

"That seems like a waste," Jax said. "A whole school shut down."

"The space was put to use," Dreema said, "just not as a school. These buildings all around us were turned into a hospital for soldiers who had been injured in the war. Some had physical injuries . . . ."

Dreema paused, and Delta leaned closer in anticipation of what she would say next.

Dreema sighed.

"Some had injuries you couldn't see."

"Like what?" Jax said. "Like cancer or something?"

"No, I mean their experiences in the war had left them with *mental* scars. Some of them were so haunted by all they had seen and done that they weren't able to return to their normal lives. So they came here. That's what happened with Private James Perkins."

"Who was that?" Jax asked.

Dreema shook her head sadly.

"Poor Private Perkins was a soldier for the Union Army. He had fought bravely in the South, participating in several battles, but he could never get over his guilt for what he had done."

"What had he done?" Delta asked in a hush.

"You know, Private Perkins went into the war understanding that he might have to kill someone. That would be hard for anyone to handle, I imagine."

Delta and Jax both nodded in agreement.

"What he hadn't counted on, though," Dreema added, "was killing a child."

"Why'd he do that?"

Jax's voice was quiet in the still night.

"Maybe it was a case of mistaken identity, or just an accident," Dreema said. "But by the time Private Perkins came to the hospital here, he believed he was being haunted by the spirit of the boy he had killed."

"Whoa!" came a small voice from the hammock.

"Private Perkins insisted that, before he was hospitalized, the ghost of the dead boy had appeared to him one night outside his tent. Just standing there staring at him."

Delta felt a chill run down her spine, but then reminded herself that it was just a story. No need to be scared. Right?

"Once he was at the hospital, Private Perkins believed he was safe," Dreema continued. "But then one night when he couldn't sleep, he decided to go for a walk out here on the Horseshoe."

Dreema looked around her and then pointed to a section of pathway not 20 feet away from them.

"Right about there," she said with certainty. "That's where he was walking when the ghost appeared again."

Delta and Jax both stared at the spot, as if the ghost would suddenly appear right then and there.

"Yes, the ghost appeared, but he soon took the form of the Private's own son, who was waiting at home for him, in a state up North. At first, Private Perkins believed the ghost was shaming him for killing another child just like his own, but within a week, he received a letter from home."

"What did the letter say?" Delta asked.

"Private Perkins' son had died of a fever," Dreema said sadly. "So now the man was mourning the death of the child he killed, and his own son."

All three sat quietly for a moment.

"Then one night, when Private Perkins was sitting on the front step of one of these buildings . . . ."

Dreema pointed to a porch nearby.

"The ghost appeared to him again, but this time it transformed into the image of his wife!"

"Don't tell me she died, too!" Jax said.

Dreema nodded.

"His wife had been so devastated by her son's death, that she went to bed and refused to eat or drink. They say she died of a broken heart."

"Sounds more like she was dehydrated," Jax said.

Delta heard Dreema stifle a laugh and then clear her throat before continuing her story.

"The very night that Private Perkins received word of his wife's death, the ghost boy appeared to the soldier at his bedside."

"'Leave me alone!' the Private pleaded with him. 'Haven't you avenged your death enough! You've taken my son and my wife! There is nothing left to take from me!'"

Dreema looked from Delta to Jax by the flickering light of the nearby gas lanterns.

"But then the ghost boy transformed one last time—into the form of Private James Perkins himself. The next morning, doctors found the Private dead in his room."

"They say that the ghost of Private Perkins still returns to these buildings, especially when kids are around. Maybe he's searching for his lost son, or maybe he wants to find the boy he killed and take revenge for the deaths of his family. In any case, don't be surprised if you wake up in your room tonight and see that you're not alone."

Delta and Jax sat quietly for a moment, absorbing all that Dreema had told them.

Finally, Jax spoke.

"Okay, but if he was dead the next morning, how did they know that the ghost appeared to him that last night?" Jax asked.

Dreema laughed.

"You got me there, Jax!"

"Yeah, it's just a story, goofwad," Delta added.

* * * *

Lying in bed in one of the old yellow brick buildings that night, Delta tried to imagine herself in that same room 150 years ago. The tan walls were maybe the same then, and the shape of the room, of course. But there wouldn't have been blinds on the windows, and there definitely would not have been a computer desk! Shut up for most of the summer, the room smelled musty and old, and if she concentrated hard enough, Delta thought she could just make out the antiseptic scent of a hospital. She closed her eyes and pictured herself as a wounded soldier, with doctors and nurses scuttling around tending to all the sick and injured patients. Patients like James Perkins.

Hearing Jax snore softly in the bed across the room, Delta sighed and rolled over with her face toward the wall. Even though she knew that Dreema had just been entertaining them earlier, Delta still was having a hard time falling asleep. It wasn't ghosts that kept her awake, though, but the sad thought of someone so tormented by the experiences of their life that they could not find peace even in death. Poor Private Perkins.

When she finally fell asleep, she had a weird dream where Pops was shooting cannons at Fort Sumter. The *Hunley* was putting across the surface of Charleston Harbor, with Tootsie sticking out the top of it waving cheerfully. Then Captain DeFoe, dressed in full pirate gear, was standing in the muddy marsh by the Island History Museum, yelling, "Get away from my ship!"

Right before Delta woke up, she dreamed she was sitting on the low-hanging live oak branch on the Horseshoe with Travis beside her. Looking up, she saw a hammock swinging in the breeze, with a boy's arm hanging over the edge. An arm with a patched gray sleeve.

What a crazy dream! she thought as she opened her eyes.

How could Delta have known that she had just taken a giant step toward unlocking the island's secret?

17

Searching the Arch

Pops was quiet on the drive back from Columbia, which Delta figured meant that the State Historical Commission had not promised to give him the money he needed for the museum. She was afraid to come right out and ask, so she just let Jax monopolize the conversation in the car. He spent most of the two-hour drive recounting the kids' campus adventures the night before and begging his grandfather to get him a hammock.

Once back on the island, Pops dropped the kids off at the house and headed to the museum.

"How was your trip?" Tootsie asked, giving each of her grandchildren a hug.

Before they could answer, though, the phone rang in the kitchen.

"I'm so sorry, sweeties," Tootsie said. "I've got to get that. I'm expecting a call about the art fair."

"No problem. We can talk later," Delta told her, heading to her room to unpack.

A few minutes later, Tootsie's voice rang through the hallway.

"Hey, kiddos! I need to go meet with a gallery owner. Want to come along?"

"To an art gallery?" Delta responded, scrunching up her nose.

"Y'all don't have to go in the gallery with me if you don't want," Tootsie said. "I thought you might like to look around the shops or visit the light-house."

"The lighthouse?" Jax asked.

"Sure!" said Tootsie. "Did I forget to mention that the gallery is in Harbor Town?"

Jax and Delta exchanged a look. They had been so focused on figuring out what "arch" meant in their old message, they hadn't really given much thought to what the "light" could be.

Of course! The Harbor Town lighthouse makes perfect sense! Delta thought.

The red and white striped tower was the logo for Hilton Head Island. Its picture appeared on everything from bumper stickers to coffee mugs to T-shirts. It had to be the "light" from their message!

"Yeah, we'll go with you, Tootsie," Delta said.

What did they have to lose?

* * * *

Tootsie parked her car under a canopy of live oak trees next to the harbor. Delta heard laughter in the distance, but then realized it was the call of gulls circling over the water.

"I bet a fishing boat just docked," Tootsie said. "Gulls are always hoping for a handout!"

The three of them walked over to the boardwalk and watched men throwing fish from the deck of a boat. Delta and Jax laughed as the gulls expertly swooped and caught each tossed treat.

"Look at the name painted on the back of the boat," Jax pointed out. "*Reel Patience*. Get it? Like a fishing reel."

They walked along the boardwalk, calling out boat names as they went. A huge yacht named *Class-Z Lady*. A tiny sailboat called *Solitude*. A fishing boat with fancy swirling letters spelling out, simply *My Boat*.

"Whoa! Look at that one!" Jax called, racing ahead.

A large boat had been decorated to look like an old pirate ship, with rope rigging and a Jolly Roger flag swaying in the warm breeze. *The Black Dagger* was painted across its side.

Delta looked beyond the *Black Dagger* and noticed that she could see the boats they'd already passed in the distance. It was as if they had been walking around the perimeter of a large circle.

"Hey, Tootsie," she said. "The harbor looks like it's perfectly round."

"Almost," her grandmother replied. "It's open to the ocean on that side over there."

Tootsie pointed to a spot in the distance. Delta followed her gaze and saw that the two ends of the boardwalk were separated by a narrow channel leading to the sea. Perched next to the channel were the red and white stripes of the Harbor Town Lighthouse.

"The harbor only forms *part* of a circle, actually," Tootsie said. "The boats are tied up here in kind of an arch, I guess."

Delta and Jax shared a look that they both understood: *We've found "the light of Hilton Head's Arch"!*

* * * *

While Tootsie headed back across the street toward the art gallery, Delta and Jax bee-lined it down the boardwalk to the base of the lighthouse. They craned their necks backward and could see an observation deck way at the top. Tiny people lined the rail, pointing out sights and taking photos.

"How do we get up there?" Jax asked.

Delta shrugged.

"There must be an entrance down here somewhere," she said.

They walked half-way around the base of the lighthouse until they came to an opened door.

Inside, the building was cramped. The ground floor had a narrow staircase against the curved wall on one side. The remainder of the room was nearly filled with a glass counter containing lighthouse-themed souvenirs. An elderly woman stood behind the counter wearing a Navy officer's uniform.

"She looks like Cap'n Crunch!" Jax whispered.

Delta shushed him and stifled a laugh as the lady gave them a dirty look.

"Do y'all have a parent or guardian with you?" she asked.

"No," Jax said.

"Our grandmother is with us," Delta corrected, suspecting that they might not be allowed up if the lady knew they didn't have an adult along. And it wasn't a *total* lie.

"She told us to go on up and she'd catch up with us," Delta said.

The lady scowled at them.

"Well, I guess it's okay if your grandma's coming soon," she said. "But be careful."

"We will," Delta answered.

As the siblings headed up the stairs, it occurred to Delta that she probably should have been calling the Cap'n Crunch lady "ma'am," like she'd heard so many folks down here say. People in Chicago didn't talk like that. If you called a woman "ma'am" back home, she'd be insulted that you were implying she was old or being sarcastic or something. Things were different down here, though. Everybody said "sir" and "ma'am" all the time like it was no big deal. As if it were expected.

Delta was starting to get dizzy as the staircase circled round and round inside the wall of the lighthouse. Now and again they would run into somebody else heading down, and Delta and Jax would have to squeeze up against the stair rail to let them pass. One of those times, Jax leaned over the rail and looked up toward the top of the building.

"How much further?" Delta asked.

"Looks like we're about half-way up," Jax said, and started climbing again.

Delta groaned. She was getting out of breath, but she guessed it would be worth it if all this effort led to a hidden treasure.

After what seemed like forever, they reached a landing at the top of the staircase and found themselves in a tiny room lined on all sides with glass. In one spot, a clear door slid open to allow access to the observation deck.

"Finally!" Jax said, and Delta couldn't have agreed more.

She was relieved to have no more steps to climb, but her relief turned to panic when she stepped outside on the deck. Her knees wobbled and her stomach felt like it was in her throat as she realized how terribly high up they were. She kept her back pressed against the wall, as far as she could get from the guard rail.

Maybe if I just look straight ahead instead of down it will be better.

Slowly, Delta focused on the distant scenery and realized she could see for miles in every direction. To one side, she saw across a golf course, past condos and woods, down the length of the island. Inching around the outside of the glass room, she watched choppy waves in the sea channel that separated Hilton Head from its nearest island neighbor, with open ocean beyond.

Delta continued on around the lighthouse until she could look down on the harbor below. Ever so slowly, she stepped closer to the rail until she spotted that fake pirate ship they had admired earlier. It looked like one of Jax's Lego models from up here, with toy-sized people walking along the boardwalk next to it. The arched shape of the marina was even more obvious from this height, which reminded Delta of why they had come to the lighthouse in the first place.

She looked over to see Jax standing a few feet away from her. He pulled the old cloth message from his pocket and started reading it again, for the hundredth time.

"So if this is 'the light of Hilton Head's arch,' then the treasure is supposed to be 'beneath' it," he said. "Like, where?"

Before Delta knew it, her brother had climbed up on the lower bar of the guardrail and was leaning over to see the ground below.

"Jax!" she cried. "Get down from there!"

A gust of wind snatched the cloth right out of Jax's hand, and off it went through the blue Carolina sky.

Before Delta could stop him, her brother had lunged forward after it, his hand catching nothing but emptiness as his body began to tip over the rail.

18

Accepting the Worst

Delta had never moved so fast! She grabbed the back of Jax's shirt and held on for dear life, yanking him backward until they both fell in a pile on the floor of the observation deck.

She lay there with her arms around her brother for a few seconds, thinking how close she had come to being an only child. As much as Jax was a pain-in-the-butt, she couldn't imagine life without him.

When her heart finally stopped pounding, though, she was just mad.

She shoved her brother aside as she sat up, then climbed to her feet and shook her hands in the air as she shouted.

"Dang it, Jax! You just about gave me a heart attack! What were you thinking? You should never lean over a high rail like that!"

A family of tourists had come rushing around the side of the glass room to see what was causing all of the commotion.

"I didn't want to lose the message," he said, hanging his head.

He had tears in his eyes, and Delta knew that he had been frightened too, maybe even more than she had been.

"Everything okay here?" a dad-looking man asked.

"Yes, sir," Delta answered. "We were just getting ready to head back down."

She took Jax by the hand and pulled him to his feet.

"Come on," she said, heading toward the sliding door that led back inside the lighthouse.

"Wait!" Jax said. "What about our message?"

Delta had forgotten what had caused all the trouble in the first place—the message had blown away!

She turned back toward the rail and carefully glanced over it. Scanning the ground below, she could see the boardwalk with some trees and flowering shrubs. People walked in small clusters here and there. How would they ever see where the message had landed?

"What if it went in the harbor?" Jax asked, sounding again like he might cry.

Delta studied the scene below, certain that the message was gone forever, until she spotted a familiar figure standing next to a palmetto tree.

Even from this height, there was no mistaking the patched gray pants and shirt, topped with a mop of curly brown hair.

"Look at that!" she said to Jax, pointing toward the boy. "That kid's following us all over the island!"

"What's his problem?" Jax said.

Just then, Patchy looked straight up toward them. Delta's first impulse was to turn away so he didn't catch her staring at him.

What the heck, she thought then. *He's the one following us, so he's the one who should feel awkward.*

She glared right back at him, until he pointed down to the ground near his feet. Lying up against the base of the palmetto trunk was a small white something. Their cloth message.

"He found it!" Jax shouted, racing toward the sliding door. "He'd better not steal it!"

The siblings scrambled down the winding stairs at three times the speed they had climbed up them. Before long, they were bursting through the doorway on the ground floor of the lighthouse and were once again out in the summer sunshine.

"This way!" Delta said, heading in the direction of the palmetto tree. She remembered it wasn't far from the fake pirate ship.

When they arrived at the tree, the piece of cloth was still there waiting for them, right where it had landed. Patchy was nowhere in sight.

"Well, at least he didn't take it," Jax said, examining the message as if it were the first time he had ever seen it.

"Yeah, well, it'll be easier—and *safer*—to look for the treasure down here, anyway," Delta said.

"The message says '*beneath*' the light,'" Jax said. "So it must be down here somewhere."

They walked all around the base of the lighthouse, but found nothing but concrete.

"Maybe it's literally 'beneath' the light," Delta suggested. "Like, inside."

She hated to have to go back inside, since the lady at the desk hadn't been especially welcoming. Even so, they needed to check it out.

"Hi, again!" Jax said, smiling broadly.

Delta hoped the Cap'n Crunch lady would follow his example and be nicer this time.

"Forget something?" the woman asked.

"No, no, just wanted to make sure we saw everything," Jax responded. "So, how long have you worked here?"

As he made conversation to distract Cap'n Crunch, Delta investigated every nook and cranny of the ground floor of the lighthouse. After a few minutes, she caught her brother's eye and shook her head.

"Well, gotta go!" Jax said, and the two kids stepped back out into the sunlight.

"Nothing," Delta said. "It was all just regular gift-shoppy stuff."

She stared absently toward the harbor, wondering where to look next, when something caught her eye. She hadn't noticed it when they were on the boardwalk earlier, but there was a large metal plaque posted about ten feet from where they now stood. Even from that distance, she could see that it included an engraving of the lighthouse.

"What is it?" Jax asked when she headed toward the plaque.

"It tells about the history of the lighthouse," Delta told him as she skimmed through the information.

It wasn't long before she sighed heavily. All hope had left her.

Jax was reading now, too, but it took him a couple of minutes to get to the news that ruined their dreams.

"1970?" he said. "This lighthouse wasn't built until 1970?"

"More than 100 years after our message was written!" Delta said. "This can't possibly be the answer to the clues."

"But it all seemed so perfect," Jax said. "The arch and the light and everything."

"Yeah, but it wasn't even here then, Jax."

The siblings sat on a nearby park bench. After a few minutes of silence, Jax spoke up.

"Hey, what about that big arched bridge over to the island? Could that be 'Hilton Head's Arch'?"

"No," Delta replied. "That bridge wasn't built until, like, I don't know. Like after Tootsie and Pops were born."

"So after the Civil War?" Jax asked.

Delta just stared at him.

"Uh, *yeah*. Way after the Civil War," she said. "And, anyway, that bridge doesn't even have any lights on it. Tootsie said there are laws on Hilton Head about keeping the lights dim so sea turtles don't get distracted by bright lights on land and wander away from the ocean or something. That's why it's always so dark around here at night."

The siblings settled back into silence, staring vacantly out at the boats bobbing in the harbor. Maybe the message wasn't even real. Or maybe whatever place the treasure was hidden didn't even exist anymore.

"I really want to help Pops save the museum," Jax said sadly.

"I know. Me too," Delta said.

She hated to even consider the possibility, but maybe the museum just wasn't meant to be saved.

She let out a heavy sigh and closed her eyes, lifting her face to the sun. The island laughed.

Delta opened her eyes with a start and then chuckled herself when she saw that the sound had come from a gull circling overhead.

Just for a second, she had thought the island itself was ridiculing them for giving up so easily in their quest to find the truth.

"We'll figure it out, Jax," Delta said. "We'll keep working at it until we do."

Delta imagined that the island smiled.

19

Spotting the Map

"Get up! Tootsie needs us to go to the store!"

Delta awoke suddenly with Jax shoving her shoulder repeatedly and yelling.

"Stop it, you little jerk," she replied, pulling the pillow from under her head and placing it over her face.

"Come on," Jax persisted. "We need syrup and Tootsie wants us to ride our bikes up to the store to get it."

"Go get it yourself, then."

Delta rolled over on her side, with her back to her brother, but he wasn't getting the message.

"You know I'm not allowed to go by myself," he said, pulling the covers off his sister.

Delta swung her arm behind her blindly. She would either grab the blankets or swat Jax—she didn't much care which. But then she caught a whiff of pancakes coming from the kitchen. She groaned and sat up in bed.

"I'll meet you out front in a couple of minutes," she said.

* * * *

Delta and Jax parked their bikes in front of the Palmetto Dunes General Store and climbed the wooden steps into the building. Delta couldn't tell whether the store was really old, or was just decorated that way. Old-timey items hung from the ceiling, and a long wooden counter stretched across the wall by the door. The store sold everything from beach pails and sunblock to fancy cheeses and wines. A section in the back had souvenirs, but Jax's favorite part was the slushee machine in the front. It was too early for slushees today, though, so they just found a bottle of pancake syrup and placed it on the counter.

"Will that be all for y'all today?" the college-aged clerk asked with a smile.

"Yeah, that's it," Delta said, digging in her pocket for the five dollar bill Tootsie had handed her as they left the house.

"Hey, Delta, look at this!" Jax said from the other end of the counter.

She looked over to see him pointing at a map of Hilton Head hanging on the wall.

"What does that look like to you?" he said.

Delta retrieved her change and thanked the clerk. She left the syrup sitting on the counter while she joined her brother. The map showed the island, surrounded by the Atlantic Ocean on one side, Skull Creek on another, and Port Royal Sound on the third. The island itself was sort of shaped like a long flat triangle, with Broad Creek cutting up through the middle of it.

"What does the island look like?" Jax repeated.

"Um, a carrot?"

"No, dummy," Jax said. "Look again."

Delta studied the map in front of her. The island wasn't really a perfect triangle, she guessed, but its shape did seem familiar somehow.

And then, all of a sudden, it struck her.

"It's a foot!" Delta said.

"Exactly!"

Jax beamed with pride at his discovery. "We're right here, in the arch of the foot!"

He pointed to a sticker on the map that said, "YOU ARE HERE!" He was right—Palmetto Dunes was smack in the arch of the foot.

But then something else caught Delta's eye. A lighthouse symbol was on the map, not far from the "YOU ARE HERE" sticker. It wasn't the Harbor Town Lighthouse, because that was clear over at the toe of the foot.

"What is this lighthouse thing supposed to be?" Delta asked the clerk.

The young woman glanced up from a magazine she was reading by the cash register.

"Oh, that's the Leamington Light. It's over on the golf course."

"A lighthouse on a golf course?" Jax asked. "Like, mini-golf?"

The girl laughed.

"No, it's a real lighthouse," she said. "It doesn't light up anymore or anything, but it's still there. It was built, like, way back. Before the Civil War, I think. They put the golf course in around it."

Delta and Jax looked at each other wide-eyed. A Civil War-era "light," in the "arch" of the Hilton Head foot!

"Hey, do you have any maps of the island for sale?" Delta asked the clerk.

"No, but we have free ones here."

The young woman reached under the counter and pulled out a sheet of paper about the size of a placemat. One side had the map of the entire island, a smaller version of the one hanging on the wall. The flip side of the paper showed a more detailed map of Palmetto Dunes Plantation. The lighthouse was clearly marked, although there didn't seem to be any roads leading to it.

"How do you get to the lighthouse?" Delta asked.

"Oh, gee," the clerk replied. "I'm not sure you can unless you're playing golf."

Jax was still examining the detailed map, though, and tracing something with his finger.

"The canal!" he whispered. "The canal leads right from Tootsie and Pops' backyard to the golf course, and then we can just cut across!"

Delta noticed the clerk giving them a weird look, so she shushed her brother. Grabbing the map, she shoved Jax toward the door and out into the sunlight.

"Thanks!" she shouted over her shoulder.

"Hey, don't forget your pancake syrup!" the clerk called.

Jax ran back in for the syrup and then met Delta by their bikes.

"This is it!" he said. "I just know this is the 'light of Hilton Head's arch' from our message!"

Delta could not disagree. All the clues were lining up. She hated to admit it, but her stupid brother may have been right all along.

Were they really going to find a treasure?

20

Meeting with Critters

By the time they got back home from the store, Delta and Jax had hatched a plan. Only golfers were really allowed on the golf course, but, technically, the kids were just going to be passing through. Even so, though, they decided to wait until dark so no one would see them. They would head out after Tootsie and Pops went to sleep tonight, and take the kayak up the canal until they got to the 8th hole. From there, it wasn't far at all to the Leamington Light. At least that's how the map made it look. They'd just have to trust that it was accurate.

"What've you kiddos got on your schedule for the day?" Pops asked as he dug into a plate of pancakes.

Delta and Jax exchanged a glance.

"Nothing," Delta said, while Jax shoved half a pancake in his mouth.

"Well, then, you should come with me," Pops said. "It's Lowcountry Critter Day at the museum. There'll be all kinds of animals there."

"Like what?" Jax asked.

"Never can tell," his grandfather replied. "Whatever the Critter King has caught this month at people's houses. Last time he had a raccoon, a snake, and an armadillo."

"So some guy just breaks into houses and steals animals?"

"Of course not, Jackson. People call him if some wild animal is being a pest, and he comes and rescues it. It's his business."

"What does he do with all the animals?" Delta asked. She pictured the man's living room, with stuffed heads hanging on plaques all around the walls.

Creepy!

"He releases them in the nature preserve over on Pinkney Island," Pops said. "But some of them he brings by the museum on Critter Day first. You should come see."

"Sounds cool, Pops!" Jax said. "Count me in!"

Delta shrugged.

"Sure, I guess," she said.

Maybe going to the museum would make the day pass faster, since she was starting to get almost excited about the adventure she and Jax had planned for tonight. She had never snuck out at night before, let alone discovered treasure.

And, anyway, Travis might be at the museum.

* * * *

The critter guy's pest-catching business must have been going strong, because he brought a whole slew of wild animals to the museum. Cages and glass tanks lined an entire wall of what used to be a dining room back when the building was used as a house. Other than Delta and Jax, though, only a handful of people had come to see the display. Pops welcomed each of them with such excitement that it made Delta sad. He seemed so desperate for the museum to succeed.

When the demonstration began, though, the animal guy (who called himself "The Critter King") acted like he was performing in front of a crowd of hundreds.

"Great to see you today, ladies and gentlemen!" he said. "Welcome to Lowcountry Critter Day, where you'll meet a variety of our island's native fauna!"

Delta scowled as he removed a fat possum from a cage and held it aloft. Its beady little eyes scanned the room as it hissed menacingly at its audience.

Ick!

He continued his presentation by showing them a fuzzy baby raccoon, a couple of turtles, and several snakes of various lengths and colors.

Jax was waiting his turn to touch a yellow corn snake when Delta felt something tickle the side of her face.

"Boo!" a voice behind her said.

She turned her head slightly to see an alligator's nose pressed up against her cheek!

"Hey!" she shouted, jumping aside and slapping at the little gator. It was just a baby, but still.

Travis laughed heartily and stroked the animal's back.

"She won't hurt you," he said. "Her teeth are just itty-bitty."

Travis was talking in a baby-voice, making sweet sounds to the gator as he held it up to his own face. Delta didn't like his attitude so much today, but at least he had sought her out and was talking to her.

"Think fast!" Travis said, and jabbed the reptile toward her face. He laughed again when she flinched.

"I wasn't scared, really," she told him. "You just startled me, is all."

The gator opened its mouth to show that its teeth were indeed small, but sharp as needles. Delta suspected that any alligator bite would hurt, no matter what size teeth it had.

"So, how's the treasure hunt going?" Travis smirked. "Found any gold doubloons yet?"

Delta hated that Travis thought she was just some dumb little kid playing a game. She had to set him right.

"Since you're so interested," she said, "it turns out there actually *is* a treasure and we're going to the Leamington Light tonight to get it."

Travis squinted his eyes at her.

"Yeah, right," he said.

Delta's head bobbed as she told him, "I *am* right, and you'll know it after I come back with a butt-load of treasure!"

Even as she said it, she knew she might be making claims she couldn't keep. What if she and Jax didn't find anything tonight? But for this moment, she had to act like it was a certainty, just to put Travis in his place.

"Whatever," he said, cradling the alligator as he turned away from Delta and sauntered in the direction of the Critter King and his menagerie.

As she watched him walk away, Delta felt an odd tingling at the back of her neck, like someone was watching her. Sure enough, when she turned around, she found that the Captain was standing against the wall, staring menacingly in her direction. Had he been eavesdropping on her conversation with Travis?

The Captain strode purposefully up to the Critter King, ignoring the children who surrounded him.

"Hey, I need your help finding my treasure," he said.

Oh no! He had *heard her talking to Travis!*

Delta rushed to find her brother. Grabbing him by the arm, she pulled him to a corner of the room.

"Jax! I think the Captain knows about Jasper's Gems!" she whispered. "We've got to find the treasure tonight before he beats us to it!"

21

Knowing That Face

Delta and her brother helped the Critter King load cages back into his truck. Jax asked a million questions about how to trap wild animals, and Delta figured he'd be spending the rest of the summer trying to catch a new pet of some sort.

After the truck pulled away, she went back inside the museum and, since Pops wasn't ready to head home yet, wandered through the exhibit rooms yet again.

There was the display on cotton, and the one on slavery. She pulled the door back and read through the info on the Battle of Port Royal again. There were some photos she hadn't really noticed before, mostly showing forts and posed-looking clusters of soldiers. Delta glanced over them and a funny thought struck her.

North or South, they all look pretty much the same. Just men in uniforms sitting around, probably wishing they were back home.

A caption near the bottom of the poster caught her eye.

"Confederate Soldiers at Ft. Walker, 1861."

Delta examined the photo. A group of soldiers, mostly in uniform, stood around a large white tent. Inside the tent, two more soldiers sat on chairs, and between them was a table draped with the Confederate flag. Fort Walker itself was not in the photograph.

Shoot, Delta thought. *I'd have liked to see what it looked like back then.*

Still, it was pretty cool that the photo had been taken the same year as their message.

As she started to turn away from the display, though, something made her return her gaze to the photo of the soldiers at Fort Walker. A familiar face.

"Jax!" she yelled.

All the other visitors had left the museum after the Critter King's show, so she wouldn't disturb anyone by shouting.

"Jax, where are you?"

"I'm coming! Geez," he said, walking into the room with his hands on his hips.

"Look at this kid in the picture!"

Delta pointed to a boy, maybe thirteen or fourteen years old, in the soldier photo. He was standing off to the side of the crowd, so she hadn't really noticed him at first.

"He looks just like Patchy!" Jax said.

Sure enough, the boy in the photo had the same curly brown hair and dark eyes as the kid who'd been following them around.

"Do you suppose this soldier kid ended up being Patchy's great-great-grandfather or something?" Jax asked.

"Maybe," Delta answered, "except it'd probably be more like great-great-great-great grandfather. This picture was taken over 150 years ago!"

"Wow!"

The siblings stood side-by-side staring at the photo, until another idea struck Delta.

"Jax, do you suppose the skeleton we found in the marsh belonged to this kid in the photo?"

"Whoa!"

"I mean, he would have been the right age, and in the right place at the right time," Delta said.

"Or, the *wrong* place at the *wrong* time!" said Jax. "Maybe Patchy knows that skeleton was his ancestor and that's why he keeps snooping around."

"But how would he know that?" Delta asked, trying to make sense of all the pieces. "And, anyway, how would the kid in the picture have grown up to have any descendants at all if he died when he was still a kid?"

Jax gave that some thought.

"Well, maybe Patchy is that guy's great-great-great-great nephew or something," he said.

"Hmm. . . ."

They continued to stare at the old photograph, lost in thought.

"You know, no matter how Patchy is related to the skeleton, what good does it do him following us around like a weirdo, anyway?" Jax asked.

Delta considered his point, and then sighed.

"Yeah, I don't know," she said. "I don't have it all figured out yet, but I feel like we're on to something."

Delta felt like the answers to the mysteries of the skeleton and Patchy were right within their grasp, like a dream that you can't quite remember after you wake up in the morning. The solution seemed almost close enough to touch. Almost.

Sneaking on Out

It wasn't until after the eleven o'clock news that night that Delta heard Tootsie and Pops turn off the television in their bedroom to go to sleep. She waited a good fifteen minutes longer before tiptoeing into Pops' den, which was serving as Jax's room for the summer. She glanced around at the floor-to-ceiling bookshelves lining the walls. The shelves held hundreds of books—all of which Pops had read—plus all kinds of cool old stuff he had collected over the years. Old Native American pottery filled one shelf, and a group of antique cameras sat on another. She noticed that her grand-father's prized saxophone sat propped in a corner, unused this summer, as if he didn't have the heart to play. Jax wasn't supposed to touch any of it, but Delta suspected that, when he was alone in the room, he did anyway.

Jax was sitting on the edge of the sofa bed, tossing his shark-teeth hatchet from one hand to the other.

"Geez!" he whispered, rolling his eyes. "I thought they'd *never* go to sleep!"

The two siblings slipped quietly through the darkened living room and into the kitchen. The vertical blinds clacked against one another as Jax reached through them to unlock the sliding glass door, and Delta grabbed them to stop their movement. They both held their breaths for a moment, listening for any sign that Tootsie and Pops had heard the noise. When all they heard was Pops' snoring, Delta slid the door open just enough for both kids to pass through and, once they were safely on the deck, ever-so-slowly pushed the door back into place.

Even though it was nearly midnight, it felt like it was 100 degrees outside. After the chill of the air-conditioned house, the humidity draped Delta like a towel still damp from the dryer. She filled her lungs with the smell of cut grass.

She caught up with her brother at the dock, where they slipped on life jackets and eased Pops' double kayak into the water and lowered themselves carefully into it. Delta sat in the back to steer, since Jax always screwed that up. Their paddles sliced rhythmically through the dark water, creating swirling eddies on the surface as they proceeded up the canal.

They weren't usually outside at this time of night—heck, they weren't even usually *awake*. Delta could hear a chorus of sounds. Night birds whooping. Frogs and crickets vying for a solo. She thought she even heard the ocean surf in the distance, but it may have just been the wind through the trees. One thing was certain, though. She did not hear any people. Folks went to bed early on Hilton Head. That would work to their advantage.

While an occasional back porch light shone dimly from the homes lining one side of the channel, the other bank was wild and woodsy. The ever-present palmettos were there, of course, some nearly as tall as a house and some just baby shrubs. Here and there a live oak tree draped a branch over the water like a fat arm dipping for a drink. Delta caught the scent of gardenia at one point, but couldn't locate the actual plant.

She stifled a scream when a rustling noise suddenly erupted from the bank next to her. The upper branches of a huge magnolia tree shook violently, and a night heron left its perch and swooped across the channel directly in their path.

"Cool! Did you see that?" Jax said in a loud whisper.

Delta took a deep breath, slapped at a mosquito, and kept paddling. She noticed a clump of Spanish moss dangling from an overhanging branch, reaching low toward the dark water. It reminded her of a spider web, and she instinctively shuddered as she passed it, sensing invisible spiders crawling over her arms.

According to the map they had gotten at the General Store, it looked like the lighthouse should be about a mile from the house. Delta figured they had gone about half that far.

A loud splash on the edge of the bank interrupted her thoughts, and Delta and Jax both froze their strokes in mid-air.

"What the heck was THAT?" Jax said.

Delta could see waves move across the water beneath the reflected stars. Something big was under that water.

"Just keep paddling!" she said, as their pace quickened. She could feel sweat dripping down the nape of her neck into the collar of her T-shirt. The hot air entered her lungs like syrup.

They moved on silently through the night.

After a while, the canal seemed to come to a dead end. Directly in front of them grew a wall of foliage that cast a long shadow over the water below.

This can't be right, Delta thought.

The canal was supposed to continue in a kind of circle all the way back around to Pops' house. It couldn't just end.

And it didn't.

As the kayak drew closer to the dark jungle, Delta saw that the water turned at a sharp, ninety degree angle to the left. To the right was their destination—the 8th hole of the Palmetto Dunes Golf Course.

Paddling toward the bank, Delta noticed a rhythmic hissing sound and hesitated.

"What's that?" she asked.

Too many weird noises out here tonight.

Jax stopped paddling and listened.

"It's just the sprinklers on the golf course, dummy," he replied.

Fountains of mist were erupting in the starlight here and there across the rolling hills of grass.

Delta let out her breath. She hadn't realized she had been holding it.

They slid the kayak beneath an over-hanging live oak and tossed the lead rope over a branch. Jax tied the rope in some overly-complicated knot he had learned at camp before climbing up onto the bank behind his sister. They quickly unfastened their life jackets and dropped them onto the grass before surveying the scene before them.

The lighthouse sat in the distance, on the edge of the golf green. They would have to go through the sprinklers, but so what? Delta's tennis shoes were already soaked from water splashing into the kayak with each pull of her paddle. And anyway, the sprinklers would probably feel great in this heat.

"Last one there's a rotten egg!" Jax yelled, running across the wet grass.

Delta started to shush him, but there was really no need to be quiet anymore. No one was around to hear them. She laughed and took off after her brother.

Jax was a good twenty feet in front of her when she noticed a palmetto shrub in her path and leapt over it. As a general rule, she was pretty co-ordinated. But as soon as her wet shoe hit the watered grass on the other side of the shrub . . . .

OOMPH!

Delta landed flat on her stomach. She had smacked her chin when she hit the ground, and could taste blood from biting the tip of her tongue. She lay there for a moment in a daze before Jax noticed she had fallen.

"Delta!" he shouted.

He's so dramatic, she thought.

She was rattled, sure. But she was basically fine. She slowly lifted herself to her hands and knees and looked up directly into a pair of yellow eyes.

From all appearances, the gator was *not* happy to be interrupted. It stood high on its legs, its back slightly arched and jaws wide open. Delta stared into its massive mouth and saw rows of conical teeth the size of her thumb. She could hear the gator's hiss over the sound of the sprinklers.

"Don't move!" Jax said. "I'll save you!"

He pulled something from the pocket of his cargo shorts. It was the little shark-teeth hatchet he and Pops had made.

Delta tried to remember anything about alligators, maybe something she had seen on TV about gator attacks, but all she could think was *ohmigod-ohmigod-ohmigod!*

The gator's yellow eyes seemed to glow in the starlight. Delta watched its eyelids slide up from the bottom and then down again.

Like some kind of alien, she thought, transfixed.

She pictured Jax having to tell Tootsie and Pops what had happened.

"We snuck out of the house in the middle of the night and now Delta is dead!" he would shout, sobbing.

With all the pressure lately, this news would push Pops over the edge and he'd probably have a heart attack and die himself. Then Tootsie would collapse with grief and never be the same again.

Mom and Dad would be heart-broken, too, of course. For the rest of their lives, they would think of Delta's tragic death every time they looked at Jax. And he would be messed up for life, having witnessed her gruesome end.

A wild thought struck her.

I'll be the talk of my school back home in Chicago. Even the cool kids will know my name. My picture will get its own page in the yearbook, as a memorial: "R.I.P. Delta Wells. Eaten by an alligator on the 8th hole of the Palmetto Dunes Golf Course."

The alligator's sudden movement snapped her back to the present.

Jax was inching toward her, but froze when the gator swung its leathery tail to the side, slapping it on the wet grass with a loud "SPLOOSH."

"I'll get him," Jax said, although his voice was shaking now.

He stepped within a few feet of his sister, holding the hatchet in his upraised hand. The gator swung its tail again, this time slapping the boy's feet right out from under him.

"Jax!" Delta screamed, drawing the animal's attention back to her. "Run!"

"But, Delta . . . ."

"GO!"

Jax half-crawled, half-ran across the wet grass until he was about twenty yards away. He stood, wide-eyed, watching his sister and the alligator. His bottom lip trembled.

The animal tossed its huge head from side to side, still showing those fearsome teeth.

Tears welled in Delta's eyes and ran down her cheeks as the gator's shoulders shifted to take a step.

This is it, she thought, adding out loud, "I love you, Jax!"

"You, too." Jax was crying openly.

Delta closed her eyes, waiting for the inevitable.

23

Staring at Death

And she waited.

"Delta . . . " Jax said slowly.

She opened one eye to see that the gator was no longer staring at her, but was focused instead on a cloud of mist right by its head. As the girl watched, the cloud became denser, until it formed a distinct figure. It was a person—a boy. A boy in tattered gray clothes.

It was Patchy.

The alligator jerked toward the ghostly image, swinging its tail wildly. *What the . . . .*

Delta blinked, but the boy in gray was still there, waving his arms in the gator's face. The huge animal directed its open jaws at the boy, seemingly forgetting about Delta.

Patchy backed toward the canal, with the gator in hot pursuit.

"Jax, are you seeing this?" Delta said to her brother.

"Uh huh."

Still frozen in a crouched position, Delta watched Patchy and the gator reach the edge of the water.

"Delta, come on!" Jax yelled.

She sprang from her hands and knees and ran as fast as she could away from the bank until she reached her brother.

Clinging to each other, the siblings stared back toward the canal, where Patchy now stood knee-deep in the water. The gator splashed around and through him, confused by its inability to catch its prey.

The boy in gray looked up and smiled at the two siblings. Then his image faded, and he was gone.

Delta and Jax stood silently for a moment, still staring at the canal. The gator had disappeared under the water and all was still now, but the siblings didn't move.

Finally, Delta spoke.

"You know that picture at the museum that looked like Patchy?" she said.

"Yeah."

"That kid in the picture didn't just *look like* Patchy, Jax—he *was* Patchy."

The mysterious boy who'd been following them all over the island wasn't just a boy. He was a *ghost!*

"So he hasn't been stalking us," Jax said, working through the details. "He's been *haunting* us!"

Jax's eyes were wide, and Delta imagined hers were, too.

"Kind of haunting us, I guess, except I don't think he's been angry at us or anything," she said. "The more I think about it, maybe he's been trying to help us find the treasure all along."

"What do you mean?" Jax asked.

"Well, you know, he's the one who showed us where the message was in the first place. You would never have found that bottle in the marsh at all if he hadn't been staring at it."

Jax nodded.

"And then, he was at Fort Walker when we were there," Delta added. "Maybe he was telling us that we were on the right track figuring out the clues."

"Yeah, and then he showed us where I dropped the message off the Harbor Town lighthouse!" Jax said.

"Right! And I remember he was shaking his head at us, like to say we were at the wrong light house."

"Well, he just saved you from an alligator," Jax said, "so I think he wants us to keep looking. We must be on the right track now!"

Delta agreed. They couldn't let anything stop them now that they were so close.

* * * *

When the siblings arrived at the foot of the Leamington Light, they were surprised to find that it didn't look anything like lighthouses they had seen before. Of course, it wasn't right on the water's edge, like most lighthouses. They had expected that. But they had figured it would look like others they'd seen, kind of decorative with a design of some sort painted around its sides.

Instead, this building reminded Delta more of pictures she'd seen of rocket ships getting ready to take off.

She leaned back and stared up toward the top of the lighthouse. She could see that the Leamington Light was much taller than the one at Harbor Town, and narrower, too. It looked like it was made of some kind of metal, because in the moonlight she could see where big bolts and rivets held sheets of it together. To support the tower, an outer skeleton of metal scaffolding surrounded it.

"'Beneath the light of Hilton Head's Arch,'" Jax said, quoting their clue. "Where do you suppose we should look?"

Delta pulled Tootsie's old phone out of her pocket and flipped it open, letting its light illuminate the ground beneath the scaffolding.

At least this old thing will be good for something!

The two kids slowly circled the lighthouse, but saw nothing to indicate a hidden treasure. They did, however, find a door in the side of the metal shaft.

"Maybe it's *exactly* beneath it," Jax said

He twisted the knob and shoved, but the door appeared to be locked from inside.

"Aw, man!" he said. "We've got to get in there somehow!"

"I think I have an idea," Delta said.

She circled the lighthouse again, looking up this time, until she found what she had spotted earlier.

"See," she told her brother, pointing skyward.

About 30 feet up the side of the tower, a dark opening was outlined against the surrounding light-colored metal. It looked as if a window had once filled the space, but now it was just a gaping rectangular hole, just big enough for a person to climb through. The surrounding scaffolding could serve as a ladder.

"I'll do it!" Jax said. "Give me a boost!"

Delta bent over at the waist and let her brother climb onto her back to reach the lowest rung of the scaffolding. That worked fine, until the kids realized that Jax was too short to reach any of the higher rungs.

"Jax, just stop," Delta told him. "You're going to fall and hurt yourself. I'll have to do it."

She sighed as she helped her brother climb back down to the ground. Delta remembered how queasy she had felt on the observation deck of the Harbor Town lighthouse. She had even been afraid to climb up to the hammock on the Horseshoe at the university. She was going to do this, though.

If there was treasure to be found—and she was really starting to believe there was—she was going to have to put her fears aside and go for it.

Delta took a deep breath and grabbed the bottom rung of scaffolding with both hands. Flipping backwards, she swung her legs up onto the bar and then pulled herself up to a seated position like she used to do on the jungle gym in the park when she was younger. Keeping her eyes focused above her, she proceeded carefully from one horizontal bar to the next, using the diagonal and vertical beams for leverage.

"You're doing it!" Jax yelled from below.

Delta resisted the urge to look down at him, knowing that she might freeze in panic if she did.

After several minutes of climbing, she could see the window not far above her. She realized with a jolt, though, that she had misjudged the distance from the scaffolding to the wall of the tower. What had appeared to be only a foot or so apart when looking from the ground, was actually more like three feet now that she could see the space between the lighthouse and its support beams.

Delta positioned herself directly across from the window. She saw that it was plenty big enough for her to get through, but her heart pounded at the thought of getting over to it. She didn't dare look down, but she knew it would be a terrible fall if she slipped trying to get across the space.

"Be careful!" Jax called. "Do it for Pops!"

Those were the last words Delta heard before she took a deep breath and dove toward the open window.

24

Digging for Treasure

Delta landed half in and half out of the window, with her waist balanced on the ledge. In the dim moonlight streaming through the opening, she could see the landing of a spiral staircase just beneath her head. Grabbing the stair rail with all her strength, she pulled the rest of her body through the window and fell with a thud on the metal stairs.

"Are you okay?"

She could hear Jax's muffled voice from outside.

Delta stood up and leaned back out the window, waving to her brother on the ground far below.

"I thought maybe you'd fallen all the way to the bottom!" Jax yelled.

Delta rolled her eyes.

"It's not like a hollow tree, stupid," she called down. "I figured there were stairs in here to get up to the light on top."

"Oh, yeah," Jax said, grinning.

Delta carefully descended the shaky old stairs, clinging tightly to the rail the whole way down. She was dizzy by the time her feet hit packed dirt, but glad to be back on solid ground.

It was nearly pitch dark at the bottom of the lighthouse, the moonlight through the window high above not reaching nearly this far down. Delta used the light from Tootsie's phone again to search the walls of the ground level until she found the doorway. She was pleased to see that the door's latch appeared to unlock from inside. She pushed on it with all her might, sensing that the door hadn't been opened in a very long time. Finally, the latch opened with a screech and Delta was able to pull the lighthouse door toward her.

"You did it!" Jax yelled, bursting into the small space and throwing his arms around his sister's waist. "I knew you could do it!"

Delta laughed and wiggled out of his grasp. The extra light through the doorway brightened the room somewhat, but Delta still held the phone screen up to illuminate their surroundings. The little area seemed to have no distinguishing features. There was no room for furniture and nothing on the walls. The floor was just hard packed dirt, except . . . .

"What's that?" Jax asked, spotting what his sister had seen.

A large flat stone was set into the middle of the floor. Aiming the light of the phone, Delta could make out some symbol carved into the rock. She brushed the years of dirt and dust off it and smiled at the familiar image.

"Hey, it's a palmetto tree and the moon," Jax said. "Just like on the flag at Pops' museum."

"It's not the moon," Delta corrected him. "Pops says that's just supposed to be a crescent shape. It stands for something, but I don't remember what."

The "palmetto and crescent" was a symbol she had seen on buildings and souvenirs all over the island. It was the symbol of the state of South Carolina.

Jax brushed more dirt from the rest of the stone.

"Whoa! Look what it says!"

Delta leaned over and gently traced a finger over the carved numbers. *"1861."*

The year that Union and Confederate forces fought at the Battle of Port Royal. The year that Colonel William Wagener wrote a message and stuffed it into a bottle. And maybe—just maybe—the year that Jasper's Gems were buried underneath the floor of a skinny metal lighthouse.

"Find something to help me pry up this stone," Delta told her brother. "I think we may have just found the 'X' that marks the spot!"

* * * *

Jax returned in less than a minute with a fist-sized rock and a rake he had found on the edge of the golf green. In the short time he was gone, Delta had scraped the dirt away all around the edges of the stone, so that its outline showed clearly in the moonlight.

"Here, I know what to do," Jax said. "I learned how to make a lever at Boy Scout Camp."

Huh. Maybe Boy Scout Camp wasn't so lame after all, Delta thought.

She watched as her brother expertly stuck the end of the rake under one edge of the stone. He then placed the rock on the ground behind it so that when he pushed down on the rake handle, the rock provided more resistance. The stone popped up enough that Delta was able to grab it and swing it to the side like a manhole cover.

She pulled the phone out again and shone the light on the space beneath the carved stone, where Jax was already digging with both hands.

"It's not packed down like the other dirt," he told Delta. "It's more sandy."

She held the phone in one hand and joined her brother's digging with the other. Neither of them spoke until Jax's hand hit something hard.

Thump!

"I found something!" he shouted.

Within seconds he was lifting something wrapped in an old piece of heavy, oily cloth. He placed the bundle gently in his lap and unfolded its cover, and Delta saw that it was a smooth wooden box about the size of her school backpack. It wasn't quite flat, but rather had a sloped top with hinges on the higher side and a lock on the other. She had seen this box before.

"What is it?" Jax asked.

"I think it's a portable desk top," she said, her voice hushed. "Remember that picture I showed you at the museum—the one of Patchy and those other guys at Ft. Walker?"

Jax nodded.

"A box *just like this one* was sitting on the table in that picture."

"Or maybe *exactly* this one!" Jax said.

He pulled at the box lid, but the lock would not budge.

"I think we're going to have to use tools or something to get it open," he said.

"We've been gone a long time, anyway," Delta said, "so I say we just take it back with us and open it there."

She had caught a glimpse of the time on the phone and realized how long they had been gone.

"Aww, but I want to know what the treasure is," Jax whined.

"We'll find out soon enough," she responded, "but if Tootsie and Pops happen to wake up and notice that we're missing, we'll be in major trouble."

Jax sighed but didn't argue.

"Go put the rake back where you found it and I'll slide the stone back in place," Delta told him.

As Jax disappeared through the door, Delta could hear him singing.

"We found the treasure! We found the treasure!"

She caught herself humming along to his tune as she replaced the stone to its original position and carefully rewrapped the box in the oily cloth. She grunted as she lifted it, wondering if the weight came from the box itself or from the magnificent jewels inside. Jax's dreams of finding treasure to save Pops' museum were coming true!

Delta was grinning widely as she exited through the lighthouse door. She turned around and balanced the box with one arm while she pulled the door shut behind her with the other.

She hadn't noticed that Jax wasn't singing anymore until she heard a deep voice from the direction of the golf green.

"Give me the box!"

She spun around, clutching the newfound treasure to her chest.

As her eyes readjusted to the moonlit night, Delta squinted and saw movement in the shadows.

She gasped as she realized what she was seeing. A tall man dressed in black, wearing a dark ski mask over his head, was standing behind Jax. Her brother's feet dangled several inches off the ground as the man held him tightly around the chest with one arm. Jax grunted and kicked his legs, struggling to get free.

"I said, give me the box," the gruff voice repeated. "Or the kid gets it!"

Delta had seen enough cop shows on TV to know what the man had in the pocket of his sweatshirt. It was shaped like a gun and was aimed right at her little brother's neck!

25

Fighting the Enemy

"Don't do it, Delta!" Jax shouted. "Don't give it to him!"

"Shut up!" the deep voice responded, shoving the gun in his pocket harder into the boy's neck.

Delta stood frozen in place, clutching the oily package to her chest. Sure, she and her brother wanted the treasure to give to Pops. They'd been working on finding it for weeks. And it could solve all of their grandfather's problems.

But it wasn't worth risking Jax's life.

"Okay, okay," she said. "Just don't hurt him."

Delta slowly stepped forward, holding the treasure box out in front of her. She didn't want to make any sudden moves that might cause the thief to do something crazy. She was leaning over to set the box on the ground when she heard Jax yell.

"No way! We found it first!"

Before Delta could say anything to stop him, her brother had reached into the outer pocket of his cargo shorts and pulled out the little shark teeth hatchet. With all his might, he slammed the jagged edge into his captor's thigh again and again.

With a pained scream, the guy dropped Jax and, forgetting whatever weapon he may have had in his sweatshirt pocket, grabbed his wounded leg with both hands. Even in the moonlight, Delta could see an even darker splotch growing on his black pants as he bled.

"What the . . . !" he said as he fell to the ground, groaning.

Delta noticed that his voice didn't sound deep and gruff anymore. Apparently, in his current state of surprise and pain, the villain had forgotten to disguise his voice as he had done before.

"Come on, Delta! Let's get out of here!" Jax yelled, running across the golf course toward the kayak moored in the canal.

She held tightly to the wrapped box and chased after him, not looking back until they were both safely in the kayak and floating through the dark water toward the house.

In the distance, Delta could make out the sound of whimpering, with the occasional curse word thrown in.

She knew that voice. She had heard it so many times, hanging on his every word. She had considered it the sweetest voice on the island.

How could you, Travis? she thought, shaking her head as they flowed farther and farther from the Leamington Light.

* * * *

The siblings were silent for several minutes, until they sensed that they were safely away from the older boy. Then Jax gave a little nervous laugh and spoke.

"Can you believe I did that?" he said.

It sounded like he could hardly believe it himself!

"You're really lucky, you know," Delta told him. "He could have shot you."

Jax laughed a bit more easily then.

"No, he couldn't have," Jax said. "He wanted us to think he had a gun in his pocket, but I could tell he was just poking me with his finger."

Now Delta laughed, too.

"What a stupid jerk!" she said.

"You don't suppose he's following us now, do you?" she added, glancing back over her shoulder.

"Not unless he wants to swim in gator-infested waters!" Jax told her. "There weren't any other kayaks by the shore."

Delta gave a small sigh of relief. She knew she wouldn't feel totally safe, though, until they were back in their grandparents' house, with the door locked behind them and the treasure safely stored. Safe from gators, ghosts, and traitorous friends.

The siblings paddled on in silence for several minutes, their strokes synchronized so that they glided smoothly along.

"Do you think that was Patchy's message?" Jax suddenly asked his sister.

"What do you mean?"

"The message in the bottle," Jax explained. "It was written back when he was alive, right? Maybe he was the one who lost it in the marsh. That's how he'd know where it was."

Delta hadn't thought of that, but it made perfect sense. And if he was the boy carrying the bottle, and the bottle was in the marsh, and the skeleton was in the marsh not far from that same spot . . . .

"Jax, the skeleton we found—it belonged to a boy about our age," Delta said. "I think it was Patchy!"

"Whoa!" Jax said. "I'll bet you're right! Remember, the first time we saw him he was watching the police gather up the bones."

"Creepy," Delta said. "Seeing your own skeleton."

She felt a surge of sympathy for Patchy. Like Private Perkins, that soldier from Dreema's ghost story on the Horseshoe, Patchy must have had some kind of unfinished business that kept him from moving on.

"Maybe he couldn't find peace after he died because he hadn't delivered the message like he was supposed to," Delta said. "You know, he was supposed to take it to some colonel at a fort over in Bluffton, and it never got there."

"Yeah, and so they never found Jasper's Gems like they were supposed to," Jax added.

"Maybe that's why Patchy wanted to help us find the treasure—so he could finish what he set out to do 150 years ago."

Jax just nodded as they slid through the creek, lost in thought.

"How do you suppose he ended up dying in the marsh in the first place?" Jax asked after a few silent moments.

"The scientist in Charleston said the gunshot shouldn't have killed him," Delta responded, "so I don't know."

"I guess we'll probably never know," Jax said.

Delta agreed, and was delighted to see that they were approaching the dock in Pops' backyard. They pulled the kayak up next to it and climbed one-by-one up onto the wooden platform. Pulling the kayak up behind them, they carefully left it with the life jackets and paddles exactly where they had found them earlier. Then they headed quietly across the lawn toward the house, Delta toting the treasure they had found.

Before they reached the back door, Jax whispered to his sister.

"Hey, Delta, you know that thing I said to you back on the golf course, when I thought the gator was going to get you?"

With all that had happened, Delta had nearly forgotten the declarations of love that she and her brother had shared when they believed all was lost.

She laughed softly and turned to Jax.

"Yeah, don't worry about it," she whispered. "I didn't mean it, either."

Delta and Jax shared a grin as they silently slid the backdoor open and slipped into the safety and comfort of their grandparents' home.

"We'll have to wait until we're alone to open the box," Delta said, and Jax nodded sadly.

She knew how he felt. It was killing her to wait, too.

What would they find when they opened Jasper's Gems?

26

Revealing the Prize

It was nearing dawn by the time the kids' excitement allowed them to fall asleep, so Delta wasn't surprised that she slept until almost noon. What *was* surprising, though, was that Tootsie had let her sleep that late!

Delta quickly dressed and wandered into the kitchen, only to find the house quiet and a note on the kitchen counter. Tootsie apparently had errands to run, and would be gone most of the day. Pops was at work, so the kids had the house to themselves. It would be a perfect opportunity to open the treasure box!

"Jax! Wake up!"

Delta shook her brother's shoulder and watched him rub the sleep from his eyes.

"Hurry up!" she told him. "Tootsie and Pops are gone for a while, so now's our chance!"

The events from the previous night registered, and Jax sprung to his feet. He had hidden the wrapped box under the couch in his room, so he dragged it out and the kids headed to the garage.

"What do you think's in it?" he said excitedly as he plopped it on Pops' workbench with a heavy THUNK.

"We'll know soon enough!" Delta replied.

They carefully peeled back the oily cloth. In the daylight, Delta could see that the wood was smooth and fine-grained. Despite the box's age, its wrapping had evidently protected it well over the years. She gently touched the old wood with her fingertips, and then noticed something that had not been visible in the darkness of night. Letters were carved into the wood in the top right-hand corner of the writing surface.

Delta traced the elaborate letters with her finger—"WW."

"Look," she said to her brother. "I think they're initials."

Jax leaned over the box and admired the fine carving.

"Jax, I think this box belonged to Colonel William Wagener!"

Delta imagined Colonel Wagener sitting at a table by a tent at Fort Walker, like in the photo they had seen at Pops' museum. She pictured him composing important documents on this very desk. And yet, at some point he had allowed the box to be wrapped in oily cloth, carried through the jungly forest, and buried in the sandy ground at the bottom of the Leamington Light.

Colonel Wagener must have believed that whatever was inside deserved to be saved. After all, he was willing to give up his portable desk to hide it. He had wanted that officer at the fort in Bluffton to find the box—to find Jasper's Gems—and if Patchy had been able to deliver his message, the gems would probably have been dug up way back then. Now, 150 years later, Delta and her brother were finally going to see what had been hidden away for so long.

The kids eyed the array of tools hanging from a pegboard on the wall over the work surface. Pops had saws, hammers, screwdrivers, wrenches, and various other contraptions that Delta could not identify.

"This should do it!" Jax said, grabbing a tool with a sharp point.

He closed one eye and, stooping low, peeked into the keyhole of the box.

"What do you see?" Delta asked.

"Nothing," he replied. "But I think I can pick the lock."

He jabbed the point of the tool into the keyhole on the lap desk and began wriggling it around randomly.

"That's not going to work," Delta said, grabbing the tool from his hand. "You're just going to break it."

She found a small-tipped screwdriver and inserted it into the hole instead. If she could just align it with the lock mechanism, a swift turn of the screwdriver might open the lock.

It didn't.

"Maybe Pops has some old keys around here that might fit," Jax said, hopeful.

He began rummaging through drawers in the workbench, looking for anything that might help.

Delta was deep in thought, staring at the box. She ran her hand around the edge of it, focusing her attention on the side opposite the keyhole. Two metal hinges sealed that side so that, when unlocked, the lid of the box could be lifted up. Delta moved in close to examine the hinges, which appeared to be attached to the wood with tiny nails.

While Jax continued his search for keys, Delta wedged the tip of the screwdriver underneath one of the hinges. She wiggled it slowly, widening the space between the metal and wood. When she had created enough of a gap, she switched tools, inserting the curved end of a hammer into the space. She had seen Pops use a hammer like this to pull nails out of wood.

"Hey, you're getting it!" Jax called, returning to his sister's side.

Delta rocked the hammer slowly back and forth until one side of the hinge popped loose from the top of the box. She looked at her brother and grinned.

"One down, one to go!"

She repeated the task on the second hinge and both kids cheered as it came loose, too. The lid of the box was now free on three sides, with only the lock holding it in place. They both stared at the task in front of them.

"Now what?" Jax asked.

Delta took a deep breath. She hated to mess up the box, but it seemed the only way to open it. And they *had* to open it. They had come too far to stop now.

She placed the box carefully on the garage floor. Slipping her fingers into the once-hinged side, she pulled the lid up enough to fit her whole hand.

"Jax! Hold the box down here, with both hands," she instructed.

The boy did as he was told, kneeling on the floor and pressing down hard on the edge of the box. Meanwhile, Delta grabbed the lid and pulled it backward with a groan. They could hear the bending of the old lock mechanism and the creaking of the straining wood.

"Delta! I can see it!" Jax shouted.

His sister stopped pulling on the box lid and squatted to see the treasure.

She could not believe what she saw.

27

Spilling Their Guts

"What is it?" Jax asked.

Well, it's not jewels," Delta responded.

She carefully reached her hand into the portable desk and pulled out exactly what anyone might expect to find. Not a treasure trove of diamonds, rubies, and pearls. No gold or silver coins.

The desk was filled with paper.

"What the heck!" Jax said.

Delta spread out the stack of brittle, yellowed papers. Some had writing on them, but most were covered in drawings. Although the ink was still dark and clear, she couldn't tell what the pictures were supposed to be. They were just outlines of shapes and stuff, not great art work of scenery or portraits. Just worthless old paper.

She looked up at Jax. He looked like he was about to cry.

"We went to all that trouble for nothing?" he said softly.

Delta didn't know what to say. She and her brother had worked for weeks to interpret the clues on the message. They had literally risked their lives to find the missing "gems." And now it turned out there were no gems at all! Not cool.

"What a rip-off!" she finally said. "We spent our whole summer looking for some stupid 'treasure' that doesn't even exist?"

"And now we can't help Pops save the museum," Jax added sadly.

Delta hadn't even thought of that. She was just feeling angry. Angry that she had wasted her summer. Angry that she had been stupid enough to be sucked in by her little brother's enthusiasm. Angry that she had ever trusted Travis.

"Ugh!" she shouted in frustration.

She picked up the hammer and tossed it downward, where it made a loud clanging noise as it hit the concrete floor.

"What in blazes is going on out here?"

Delta quickly looked around the garage to see her brother stooped over the bent old portable desk, the yellowed papers it had once held spread all around him.

And in the doorway to the house, Delta's grandfather stood with a scowl.

* * * *

"What are you kids doing out here in my garage?" Pops asked "You know you're not supposed to play with my tools when I'm not around."

"We weren't playing, Pops," Jax said. "We were trying to save the museum."

Delta saw her brother's bottom lip begin to quiver.

"Save the museum?" their grandfather said. "What are you talking about?"

Delta sighed and looked at her brother.

"We might as well tell him now," she said with a shrug.

Jax was too near tears to talk.

"Okay," she began. "It all started after we found the skeleton in the marsh."

Pops was listening attentively, his hands on his hips.

"Remember that next day, when all those people came to the museum property to see the site? After we'd been in the paper?"

Pops nodded.

"Well, Jax found an old bottle in the marsh that day, not far from where we'd found the skeleton," Delta explained.

"I was going to give it to you for your birthday," Jax said. "I know you like old glass."

"But then I accidentally broke the bottle," his sister said. "And I thought Jax would be mad at me but he wasn't, because there was a message inside the bottle."

"A really old message," Jax inserted, the excitement of the story replacing his urge to cry.

"Yeah, it was from 1861," Delta said.

"1861?"

Pops was clearly even more interested in the story now that it had taken a historic turn.

"Wait! I'll show you," Jax said, pushing past his grandfather and heading down the hallway toward his bedroom.

Jax returned a minute later waving the no-longer-so-mysterious message. Pops took the cloth and carefully examined it, his eyes gleaming.

"'November 7, 1861'," Pops read. "Why, that's the date of . . . ."

"The Battle of Port Royal," Delta said, nodding.

She pointed to the name at the bottom of the message.

"And Colonel William Wagener was the officer in charge of Fort Walker," she added. "He died later that night in the battle."

Pops smiled and shook his head.

"Why didn't you kiddos show me this sooner?"

"It was going to be a birthday surprise," Jax said, frowning. "But then the treasure turned out not to be a treasure at all."

"Wait, what?" Pops said. "Treasure?"

Delta nodded.

"We wanted to find 'Jasper's Gems' for your birthday," she said. "And we thought the money from the treasure might save the museum."

Pops smiled.

"But, honey, 'Jasper's Gems' aren't real jewels," he said.

"We know that now," Jax responded, rolling his eyes.

"Yeah, we figured out that this clue here . . . ."

Delta pointed to another spot on the message.

"'The light of Hilton Head's arch.'" she said. "We figured out that Colonel Wagener meant the Leamington Light."

"Because the Harbor Town light is too new, even though the harbor looks like an arch," Jax added. "But then we saw a map of the island at the store, and I showed Delta how Hilton Head is shaped like a foot."

"That's right," Delta said. "And the Leamington Light is in the arch of the foot."

Pops was looking from one of them to the other and then back down at the cloth message still in his hand.

"You figured this out all by yourselves?" he asked.

"Sure," Jax said. "And then when we got to the Leamington Light. . . ."

"Whoa there," Pops said, putting his hand up in a "stop" signal. "You actually went looking for a treasure?"

"Yes, sorry, Pops," Delta said, looking toward the ground. "We took your kayak and cut across the golf course."

"But we put everything back right where we found it," Jax quickly added. "We didn't hurt your kayak or your paddles or anything."

"Right," Delta agreed. "And inside the lighthouse, on the floor, we found this flat stone with the South Carolina symbol on it . . . ."

"You know, the palmetto tree and the moon," Jax interrupted.

"Palmetto tree and *crescent*," Delta corrected. "Anyway, '1861' was carved on it, too, so we figured that was the right spot. So we pushed the stone aside and dug up, well, that."

Delta motioned toward the bent-up portable desk sitting on the garage floor.

For the first time, Pops noticed the mess of papers, oily cloth, and wooden box. He walked toward it and stooped down slowly, as if in a daze.

"You kids dug this up from under the lighthouse?" he said softly.

"It was wrapped in that tarp, but don't touch it," Jax said. "It's all greasy."

"It's oil cloth," Pops said. "It's waterproof, so it helped preserve the box."

He gently ran his hand over the smooth wood of the desk.

"I'm sorry we bent the lid back," Delta said. "We couldn't get the lock to open, so I took the hinges off. But then we still had to bend it to see what was inside."

"We thought it was going to be treasure," Jax said gloomily.

"One kind of cool thing, though," his sister said.

She pointed out the carved initials on the lid of the box.

"I think this might have belonged to Colonel Wagener, since it says 'WW.'"

Pops traced the initials with his finger and smiled.

"We're real sorry we couldn't find you treasure," Jax said. "All that was in it was a bunch of old papers."

The kids' grandfather focused his attention on the drawings on the floor, examining them each, one by one. Finally, he looked up at Delta and Jax.

"Do you kids know what you've done?" he said.

Reliving the Past

Delta and Jax both swallowed hard, bracing for major trouble.

Pops' face burst into a wide grin.

"You've found 'Jasper's Gems'!" he said.

The siblings looked at each other, worried. Had the stress of this summer, with the threat of the museum closing and all, finally caused their grandfather to crack?

"But, Pops," Jax said slowly, "there are no gems."

Pops laughed and held up a sheet of yellowed paper in each hand.

"These are 'Jasper's Gems'!" he said. "Julius Jasper was a designer of submarines."

The kids stared at him in confusion.

"Remember when we saw the *Hunley* in Charleston?" Pops asked.

Delta and Jax nodded, still not understanding.

"Remember how I told you the *Hunley* was so innovative because submarines had never been used in wartime before?"

"Yeah, but the *Hunley* sank three times," Delta said.

"Exactly!" Pops replied, smiling again as he looked back over the drawings. "Ever since the Civil War, there has been a myth of sorts that Julius Jasper had invented an improved type of submarine—one that didn't have the problems that the *Hunley* did."

"But Julius Jasper died on the *Hunley*," Delta said.

"That's right," Pops said, seemingly impressed that his granddaughter knew that fact. "So no one ever knew what happened to his plans for that sub, or if they even existed. After so many years, most historians figured that 'Jasper's Gems' were just a legend. But now here they are, spread across the floor of my garage!"

He looked again at the display of papers spread around him, shaking his head and grinning.

"You know, there are better submarines now, Pops," Jax said. "Like nuclear ones. Somebody did invent a better sub than the *Hunley*."

His grandfather laughed.

"I know that, Jackson. These plans won't likely be made into real submarines. But their historical value is priceless! They are a missing link of sorts from the history of our country."

"So, in a way," Delta said, "they really are a treasure?"

"A wonderful treasure!" Pops said.

Delta and Jax looked at each other in relief and grinned. It looked like all their troubles hadn't been for nothing after all!

Jax stepped over and patted his grandfather on the back.

"Happy early birthday, Pops!"

* * * *

Later that afternoon, Tootsie sat at the kitchen table laughing as Delta, Jax, and Pops all talked over each other, sharing their exciting story. The kids specifically neglected to mention the part where Delta had almost been eaten by an alligator. In their happiness about "Jasper's Gems," Tootsie and Pops hadn't mentioned any kind of punishment for the kids, but Delta figured that their grandparents might change their tune if they thought the kids had been taking actual life-threatening risks.

Jax did tell them about his run-in with Travis, though.

"How did he know to find you at the lighthouse?" Tootsie asked.

"I told him we were going there," Delta said. "When I saw him at the museum yesterday."

"You told him?" Jax said. "But it was supposed to be a secret!"

"I know, but he was teasing me about finding 'gold doubloons' and stuff, and I just kind of wanted to put him in his place."

Delta rolled her eyes.

"I should never have cared what he thought of me," she said. "He's such a jerk."

"He thought he was so tough, but I knew he couldn't hurt me," Jax said. "Not when I had my shark-teeth hatchet!"

"What?" Tootsie said.

"Yeah, I hit him in the leg a few times with my hatchet and he was afraid to mess with us after that!"

"Now, Jackson," Pops said seriously. "I helped you make that hatchet as a craft and history lesson. You know you weren't supposed to actually use it to hurt anyone."

"But I needed it for self-defense," Jax argued. "If I hadn't used it, Travis would have stolen 'Jasper's Gems'!"

"Well, I don't want to hear of you using it as a weapon again," his grandfather said. "Is that clear?"

"Okay," Jax replied, but then added, "Hey! We almost forgot to mention Patchy!"

Delta shot her brother a look that siblings understand to mean, "Keep your mouth shut!"

Tootsie and Pops were impressed with the kids' bravery and cleverness in finding the treasure, but they would never believe that Delta and Jax had been seeing an actual ghost all over the island!

"Who's Patchy?" Tootsie asked.

"That's the name we gave the boy in the photo at the museum," Delta answered quickly before her brother could speak.

"There was this old photo taken at Fort Walker in 1861, with men around a tent," she added.

"I know that photo," Pops said thoughtfully. "Isn't there a portable desk on the table in that photo?"

"Uh huh, maybe the same desk we found," Jax said.

"Anyway, we noticed that there's a boy in that photo who looks about my age. His clothes were all patched up, so we named him 'Patchy,'" Delta continued. "And it occurred to us that maybe he was the kid whose skeleton we found."

"Well, maybe."

Pops did not sound convinced, but Delta couldn't tell him about the ghost boy who had helped them solve the clues, how he had first appeared right after they found the skeleton. That he showed them where the old glass bottle was hidden in the marsh.

It was enough that she and her brother knew the truth.

As Tootsie stood up to start preparing dinner, she noticed something lying on the kitchen counter.

"What's this?" she asked.

"Oh! In all the excitement, I almost forgot!" Pops said. "You two kiddos got some mail at the museum today."

He gestured toward a fat envelope lying on the kitchen counter.

Who would be sending Delta and Jax mail to the Island History Museum?

29

Opening the Mail

Delta picked up the envelope and examined it. Her and Jax's names were centered on the front in neat handwriting. In the return address corner, Delta saw a single word.

"Dreema"

"Hey, it's from that grad student at USC!" she said.

"What would she be sending us?" Jax asked.

"I don't know," Delta responded.

She ripped the envelope open and found several sheets of paper folded together inside.

"What's it say?" Jax asked, leaning against his sister to get a better look. Delta began reading the first page.

Hi, Delta & Jax!

Thanks again for spending the evening with me while you were in Columbia. I had a blast and hope you did, too!

Remember that story I told you about Private Perkins? You'll never guess what I found out about him! While doing my grad research, I came across some pages from his diary that the university had filed away. It turns out that he really was a patient here when the campus was used as a hospital. I have sent along copies of a section of his diary where he talks about some time he spent on Hilton Head. Since you're spending your summer there, I thought you might be interested in seeing it. Spoiler alert, though— what Private Perkins wrote is really sad. ☹

Stop by and see me next time you visit Columbia!

Your friend,

Dreema ☺

"Wow!" Jax said. "So that ghost story was true!"

"Well, it was about a real guy, anyway," Delta said, flipping to the pho-
tocopied pages that Dreema had included with her letter.

It was obvious that the copies were of a very old piece of writing. She
could tell that the pages were discolored, and the original paper looked
like it was worn a bit around the edges. Although the ink was still dark
and clear, Delta had to strain to interpret the swirly handwriting, since she
seldom used cursive herself.

Tootsie and Pops sat at the kitchen table and listened along with Jax as
Delta read the diary pages aloud.

April 20, 1862

*Yet again, I cannot sleep tonight. Although it has been months since my
brief time on Hilton Head Island, I am still haunted by guilt for what I did
there. As a soldier devoted to my country, I had prepared myself for the
possibility of killing a man in battle, but what I did goes beyond killing, and
it did not involve a man. It is as if I relive that night over and over again.*

*It is the evening of November 6, 1861, and my troop arrives by ship at
Hilton Head Island, where we invade Fort Walker on the island's northeast
tip. I am directed by my commanding officer to locate and capture the
fort's leader, a certain Colonel William Wagener. A fellow soldier approaches
the Colonel's tent with me, but as we round the corner of the tent, I see the
Colonel hand a whiskey bottle to a boy in his service. He shouts at the boy
to "Get this to Bluffton," and the boy takes off like a shot through the surrounding forest.*

*"I'll get the Colonel. You get the boy!" my fellow soldier shouts, so I fol-
low the boy to prevent his getting help.*

*Although I am a grown man and he is probably no more than 12 or 14
years of age, he is fast and I find myself breathing heavily as I chase the
boy through woods so thick I can barely see the full moon shining overhead. The boy leaps over fallen logs and waves away vines without slowing,
and I fear he will get away from me and warn a nearby camp. So I do what I
feel I have to do, but I do it mercifully.*

*I shoot the boy in the leg. I do not shoot to kill. After all, I have my own
boy at home nearly that age, and I would not harm one hair on his head. I
did not come to this war to murder a child. But I do shoot that boy in the
leg to slow him down.*

And he does begin to limp, but he keeps running. I can see his dark shadow moving ahead of me through the forest, and I keep up with him as best I can. But then I see a brightness ahead that blinds me somewhat and pretty soon I do not know where that boy has gone. I keep running forward, toward the light, and soon find myself arriving on the banks of a salt marsh. I can see then that the light is from the moon itself, and I can hear splashing in the distance.

In the light of the moon, I can just make out the boy, partially hidden by waving grasses. Although he is only a few yards from the bank, he appears to be in deep water, since I can only see his shoulders and head above the surface. Oddly, though, he is no longer moving through the water trying to get away. I take a step toward him, but my foot sinks into the wet mud of the bank up to my knee. I am able to pull myself out, but realize then that the boy cannot. He is stuck in that marsh mud, sunk up to his chest.

I do not know what to do. If I go in after him, I might get stuck, too. There is a tree near the bank with a low-hanging branch, and I sit on that branch wondering what to do next. The boy watches me, too, waiting to see what I will do. But I soon realize I will have to do nothing.

As the time passes, I can see that the tide is coming in. It laps farther up the bank and I can see that it now reaches the boy's chin. I can tell where the high tide line is by the smoothness of the bare mud, and it still has a ways to go. I feel a sickness in my belly as it dawns on me that the boy is stuck in that rising tide, and that pretty soon it will cover him completely. Unless I do something to save him, he is going to drown.

I think of my own son at home, and I sit on that tree branch and sob like a baby. The water is up to the boy's nose now. In the moonlight, I can see he has his head tilted way back so as to keep breathing as long as possible.

I sit there on that tree branch and watch the tide rise to the top of that boy's head, until finally the water covers him completely and I know that he will not be taking any warning to Bluffton or anyplace else.

Afterwards, I head back to Fort Walker to find that we have been triumphant. Fort Walker and Hilton Head Island are now under Union control. We celebrate our victory the rest of that night and the whole next day.

But what I did on the edge of that marsh changed me. The choices I made there have left me a mere shell of the man that I was before. I did not kill a man in battle. I sat and watched a child die a slow and horrifying death. And I did not do one thing to stop it from happening.

Now, months later, I fear that the awful sin I committed is one that cannot be forgiven, not by my family, not by myself, nor by my God.

How am I to live with this guilt?

The room was silent as Delta finished reading. Finally, Jax spoke softly. "That was Patchy that drowned, wasn't it?"

Pops cleared his throat.

"Well, it certainly explains a lot about the skeleton you found," he said.

"That poor boy!" Tootsie added. "Can you imagine how terrified he must have been?"

"Do you think Private Perkins could have rescued him?" Delta asked. "I mean, if he had tried?"

Pops shook his head as he answered.

"It's hard to say. He could have gotten stuck, too, I suppose, although he could have just gone out part way and extended a branch or vine or something for the boy to grab on to."

"But they were enemies," Jax said. "Soldiers don't usually help their enemies during a battle."

"I think Private Perkins believed he could have saved Patchy," Delta said. "Or why else would he feel so guilty?"

Everyone nodded at that.

"When we were at USC, Dreema told us about the legend of Private Perkins," Delta explained to her grandparents. "In that story—which we all thought was completely made up—Private Perkins ended up haunted by the ghost of a boy he killed during the war."

"Then, it was true!" Jax shouted. "I bet he really did see Patchy's ghost!"

"Perhaps the legend exaggerated the history a bit," Tootsie suggested with a smile.

"That's right," Pops said. "You know, the best stories combine a bit of the truth with a bit of imagination."

"Well, what's happened to us this summer is true," Jax said, "but it's so crazy nobody's ever going to believe it!"

Celebrating with Friends

Delta couldn't believe how fast everything started changing after she and Jax came clean with Pops and Tootsie about what they'd been doing all summer. Not only was Pops thrilled to see Julius Jasper's missing submarine designs, but the State Historical Commission was excited about the discovery, as well. In fact, they proposed to Pops that he create a new exhibit about Civil War submarines at the Island History Museum, featuring "Jasper's Gems." That display would be just a small part of the new "Hidden History of Hilton Head" room at the museum, which would introduce visitors to the Legend of Private James Perkins, the tragic story of Patchy, and of course the discovery of the skeleton in the marsh.

Newspapers and television news stations throughout South Carolina, North Carolina, and Georgia had covered the exciting story of Delta's and Jax's treasure hunt, and all the publicity was already drawing visitors to the museum, even though the new exhibits weren't even completed yet.

With all the new interest in the museum, Delta shouldn't have been surprised when Pops came home literally cheering one day.

"Woohoo!" he shouted as he burst through the door. "The Historical Commission is giving us the money we need to run the museum!"

Tootsie squealed and threw her arms around her husband.

"Between the money and the new visitors, it sounds like the museum is saved!"

"You bet it is!" Pops said, kissing her loudly on the cheek. "And donations have been flowing in all week from people and companies that heard our story on the news and want to support our cause!"

Delta watched her grandparents dance a waltz around the kitchen, even though there wasn't any music. She laughed along with them as it occurred to her that this was the happiest she had seen them all summer long.

One evening about a week after their adventures at the Leamington Light, Delta and Jax helped Pops celebrate his birthday on the grounds of the museum. The whole staff had turned out for the party, happy to honor their boss and friend.

"Well, it looks like my grandkids aren't the only ones who found 'treasure'," Pops said with a grin.

Delta looked over to see a pleasant-looking elderly man approaching. She didn't recognize him at first, what with his khaki pants and clean shirt. His hair was tidy and his beard was trimmed. If it hadn't been for the hook hand, she wouldn't have known it was Captain DeFoe at all.

Well, that and the parrot on his shoulder.

"Yep!" the Captain said, with a big smile. "I sure am glad to have her back!"

Seeing the kids' confusion, Pops turned to them and explained.

"This is Captain DeFoe's pet bird, Treasure. She's been missing for the past few weeks."

"That's right," the Captain said. "Usually she's real well-behaved outside, but a big gull came into my yard one day and Treasure flew right off my shoulder to chase him. I kept thinking she'd just fly back, but after a couple of weeks I had about given up on her. Broke my heart, too. I've had that bird for over 20 years."

"How did you end up finding her?" Tootsie asked.

"I got the Critter King to help me," the Captain replied. "He gave me some tips on luring her back, and within a few days—well, there she was! I guess she finally got homesick."

Delta recalled with new understanding the interaction she had witnessed on Lowcountry Critter Day.

"*I need your help finding my Treasure.*"

The Captain hadn't been asking the Critter King to find Jasper's Gems. He had wanted help finding his lost pet!

The old man looked lovingly at the parrot, stroking her feathers gently.

"Well, I sure am glad to see you back to your old self again," Pops said.

"I know, and I appreciate your patience with me while she was missing. Treasure's like family to me, you know."

Pops nodded and the old man walked off to mingle with other guests.

"Well, what do you know?" Jax said. "I guess 'Treasure' is a perfect name for a pirate's parrot."

"A 'pirate's parrot'?" Tootsie said. "What are you talking about, Jax?"

"Well, not a *real* pirate. A guy who *thinks* he's a pirate, I mean."

Pops and Tootsie both looked totally confused.

"Jackson, *who* thinks *who* is a pirate?" Pops asked.

Delta spoke up.

"It's okay, Pops. We know the truth."

"What truth?" her grandfather asked, looking from Delta to Jax for explanation.

"About the Captain," Jax whispered. "We know about him being a murderer and in an insane asylum and everything."

"What?" Pops said so loudly that other people turned and looked at him. "What in the world are you two talking about?"

"You know, how the Captain used to be a fisherman, but then he went crazy after he was lost at sea," Delta said. "He thought he was a pirate, and cut off his hand and killed all those other fisherman."

Hearing herself say it out loud, and watching the amazed expressions on her grandparents' faces, Delta suddenly realized how ridiculous the story sounded. If anyone other than Travis had told her, she would never have believed it in the first place. But she had wanted so badly to believe in him.

Tootsie and Pops both burst out laughing.

"Where did you hear that tall tale?" Tootsie asked.

"Travis told us," Jax said in a small voice. "He said you didn't tell us yourselves because you didn't want us to be scared."

Pops put an arm around each of his grandchildren.

"Well, kiddos, it seems Travis was just messing with the two of you," he said. "Captain DeFoe is as harmless as a housecat."

"But you told us to stay out of his way," Jax said.

"Well, sure," Pops responded. "He's a busy man when he's at work. He didn't need you kids underfoot. Plus, he was having a hard time with his bird gone missing and all, and that made him kind of grumpy."

"Not just a bird, Pops. A *parrot*—a *pirate* bird," Jax said. "And we saw him drinking rum."

Tootsie handled this one with a chuckle.

"Jax, honey, lots of people have pet parrots. And you don't have to be a pirate to drink rum."

"But he called that model ship 'my ship'," Jax said, sounding less sure all the time.

"That's because he built the model, Jackson," Pops told him. "Model ship-building is a hobby of his. Has been for years."

"So, he didn't spend time in an insane asylum or kill a bunch of people?" Delta asked.

"A definite 'no' to the insane asylum. The other part is kind of complicated," Pops said, growing serious.

"What do you mean, 'complicated'?" Jax asked. "He *did* kill those fishermen?"

"No, no, of course not!" Pops said. "Captain DeFoe is one of the best, most honorable men you'll ever meet. In fact, he's got a whole slew of medals to prove it."

"Medals?" Delta asked.

"That's right. He was a Captain in the United States Marine Corps during the Vietnam War. Served several tours of duty over there and saved the lives of many of his fellow soldiers," Pops said. "Unfortunately, though, part of war is often killing enemy soldiers, and I'm afraid the Captain had to do that to save his own life and those of his troops."

Delta and Jax listened wide-eyed.

"During one battle, Captain DeFoe got his hand blown off while he was saving another man. That's why he has the artificial hand," Pops said. "That's also what earned him the Purple Heart medal."

"The Captain is a real American hero," Tootsie added.

Wow! Delta couldn't believe how wrong they had been about the old guy. But then, she couldn't believe how wrong she had been about Travis, either.

Suddenly, a loud noise erupted from across the yard and everyone looked toward the sound. Travis was under a giant magnolia tree, limping wildly in a zigzag pattern and screaming at the top of his lungs. Treasure flew a few feet over the teenager's head, flapping her wings just out of reach of Travis's flailing arms. The bird's squawks blended with the crowd's laughter so that it seemed everyone involved—except Travis—was enjoying the excitement.

"Pops, I'm surprised you didn't fire Travis after what he did at the lighthouse," Delta said.

She could see the bandage on Travis's leg, sticking out from beneath his shorts as he tried to run from the parrot. His limp made it clear that Jax's little shark teeth hatchet had done its job protecting her and her brother.

"Well, I certainly considered it," Pops said with a sigh. "But then I decided he shouldn't get off that easy."

"What do you mean?" Jax asked.

"I had a little talk with Travis and his father, and we all agreed that I would not press charges against him for what he did so long as he worked for the museum *without pay* for the rest of the summer."

"They agreed to that?" Delta said.

"Let's just say he's not here for the party today!" Pops said.

III

Delta glanced back toward Travis and saw that Treasure had returned to the Captain's shoulder. While the others gathered there that day were celebrating the museum's promising future, Travis was stuffing fallen magnolia leaves in a large plastic garbage bag.

"Why did he even need the treasure?" Delta asked. "Isn't his family already rich? I mean, he said he went to boarding school in Charleston, so I just figured."

"He didn't want any treasure for himself," Pops explained. "He just didn't want *you* to find it and use it to save the museum."

"But wouldn't he want to save the museum, too, since he works here?" Jax said.

Pops chuckled.

"He only worked here to spy on us for his dad," he said. "You see, his father's development company was the one trying to turn the museum into a resort."

"So he's probably not in the mood to celebrate today, anyway!" Tootsie said.

"Well, I am!"

Jax sprinted toward the food table, eyeing the feast of barbecue, fried chicken, macaroni and cheese, potato salad, deviled eggs, and every type of cake, pie, and cookie imaginable. There would be a watermelon-eating contest later, and Delta could hear the electric whirr of a machine making homemade ice cream.

She glanced over at Tootsie and Pops, standing arm-in-arm, surrounded by friends who shared their joy and excitement about the museum. This was the happiest she had seen her grandparents all summer—maybe ever.

The sun was high, but the ancient live oak trees shaded the lawn of the old building. The air was heavy with the scent of gardenia and pine. Delta breathed in deeply.

What a summer!

Pops strolled over to join his granddaughter. Standing next to her, taking in the joyful scene, he placed an arm around her shoulder.

"Been anytime interesting lately?" he said.

"Oh, about 150 years ago," Delta said with a smile. "Right here on this very island."

* * * *

The sun was going down and still Pops' birthday party was in full swing. The older folks were dancing, so Delta and Jax decided to go for a walk.

Delta could hear the sounds of laughter and Pops' saxophone music on the grounds of the Island History Museum as she and her brother strolled down the dirt road toward the tidal flats.

When they reached the bank of the marsh, small waves lapped gently upon the shore and sea grasses swayed softly in the breeze. The air smelled of salt and pluff mud, and Delta saw a fish jump out in the creek and land with a splash right about in the spot where yellow "crime scene" tape had been stretched just a few short weeks earlier. Where, more than 150 years ago, a boy not much older than Delta had been courageous, and yet had died. Where, that same night, a soldier had struggled to balance being true to his country with being true to himself.

Now, though, it was as if nothing special had ever happened there.

Delta stood on the bank and watched her brother search for oyster shells in the mud.

"Remember the first time we came out here this summer?" Jax asked.

"Uh, *yeah!*" his sister said. "I'll never forget that day as long as I live. You have no idea how creepy it is to stick your hand in somebody's skull!"

Jax laughed at that, but then turned serious.

"I hope Patchy knows that he *did* deliver his message, even though it took him a lot longer than he expected."

Delta nodded. She thought of Private James Perkins, who continued to haunt the Horseshoe at the university because he could not find peace. His unfinished business had ruined his life—and his death, too. She hated to think that Patchy would spend eternity wandering like that. She hoped that she and her brother had helped him find peace.

And then she knew they had.

"I'm pretty sure he's ready to move on," she said with a smile.

She nodded toward the marsh of Broad Creek, and Jax's eyes followed her gaze.

In the shallows, just a few feet in front of the siblings, stood a boy in baggy gray clothing with patches on his shirt. His hair was still shaggy, but his eyes were no longer serious and sad.

Patchy smiled at his two friends, and then turned and waded into the water. He walked until the water reached his chest, and then he turned back toward the shore.

Without thinking, Delta raised her hand in a wave to the boy only she and her brother could see.

"Bye, Patchy!" she whispered.

The boy in gray raised his hand in reply and, with a nod and a smile, slowly transformed into a mist that simply faded away under the light of the moon.

"Is it weird that seeing him isn't even weird anymore?" Delta asked, still staring out at the water.

"I know," Jax replied. "I've finally gotten used to the idea of seeing a ghost, and now we'll probably never see him again."

"I'll kind of miss him," Delta admitted, as the siblings turned and headed back in the direction of the party.

As they trudged back up the road from the marsh, Delta glanced down and happened to catch a glimpse of her brother's feet.

"Um, Jax," she said. "Where's your other shoe?"

FACT OR FICTION?

Even though *The Sea Island's Secret* is a fictional novel and Delta and her family are inventions of the author, there are many places, characters, and historical events mentioned in the story which are actually real.

🔍 Hilton Head Island is a real foot-shaped island off the coast of South Carolina. Just like in *The Sea Island's Secret*, it has beaches, marshes, golf courses, and even wild alligators.

🔍 Pops' Island History Museum is based on the Coastal Discovery Museum, which is a real Hilton Head attraction. In addition to indoor and outdoor nature and history exhibits, it has a butterfly house, walking trails, beautiful gardens, and scenic views over the marsh. It also offers classes and island tours for visitors of all ages.

🔍 The Battle of Port Royal really did take place near Hilton Head on November 7, 1861. Fortunately, though, few soldiers were actually killed in the battle. Instead, the Confederate Army realized they were outnumbered and fled to the mainland. They peacefully turned over Fort Walker to the Union Army, which ended up controlling Hilton Head Island and Port Royal for the rest of the Civil War.

🔍 The Civil War really did divide families, just like Pops told Delta, with relatives often fighting for opposing sides. In the Battle of Port Royal, for instance, the leader of the Confederate forces at Fort Walker was Brigadier General Thomas Drayton. Meanwhile, the Union Navy forces attacking the fort from Port Royal Sound were led by Captain Percival Drayton—Thomas's own younger brother!

🔍 Both the Harbor Town Lighthouse and the Leamington Light are real and can be found just where Delta and Jax saw them. However, the Leamington Light was actually built by the Union Army after it took control of the island. The Light would not have existed at the time of the battle, so the treasure could not have been hidden there.

🔍 "Jasper's Gems" were a figment of the author's imagination, although the *H. L. Hunley* is a real submarine that did sink three times during the Civil War. It sank for good in 1864 after torpedoing and sinking the Union ship USS *Housatonic* outside of Charleston Harbor, making it the first submarine in history to sink an enemy ship. Since its discovery on the bottom of the Atlantic Ocean in 1995, it is now being restored at the Warren Lasch Conservation Center in Charleston, South Carolina.

🔍 The buildings on "the Horseshoe" at the University of South Carolina really were used as hospitals for both Confederate and Union soldiers during the Civil War. Some buildings are said to be haunted by the spirits of these former patients. What do you think?